Property

PROPERTY

A Novel by
Marc Diamond

Coach House Press
Toronto

Special thanks to Kugler, editor, and Penelope, muse.

Published with the assistance of the Canada Council,
the Ontario Arts Council and the Ontario Ministry of
Culture and Communications.

Canadian Cataloguing in Publication Data

Diamond, Marc Leslie, 1944-
Property

ISBN 0-88910-436-0

I. Title.

PS8557.I35P7 1992   C813'.54   C92-093316-5
PR9199.3.D53P7 1992

Dedicated to the memory of Michael Diamond

Mail must be coming, I think. Mail! Mail! Mail! News!
Some day a message must come that won't disappoint me.

—Thomas Bernhard, *Gargoyles*

The envelope containing the letter came through the slot, floated down, hit the wood floor with a muffled slap, the sound of a gloved hand striking a face. I observed this descent, this unwelcome confirmation of the inevitable laws of gravity. I saw it. I happened to be staring at the front door of my house in Vancouver, a house that is not my house, it really belongs to the bank, most of it, but I live there, I pay the bank for the privilege of living there, and I am grateful. I happened to be sitting motionless on the wood floor of the hallway, staring at the front door, my hands grasping my bent knees. This is not unusual. It is my nature to fix on some object and regard it for a long period of time; it is my nature to be motionless for a long period of time. But now the letter was marring the serenity of the polished wood floor, and I was impelled, against my nature, to go to it and remove it from the field of view. I stood, took steps, leaned over the letter and read the return address: Robert Crow, 97 Blackpool Drive, London Ontario. This disturbed me. In fact it ruined my day. Anything to do with London Ontario ruins my day. As soon as the existence of London Ontario is brought to my consciousness, it ruins my day. If I think even for a moment of London Ontario, or hear it mentioned on the radio, or read of it in the newspaper, my day is finished. I may as well go to bed, not that going to bed would help, for once it is in my mind there is no escape from London Ontario, from those twisting streets, sleep is impossible, and even if I did go to bed, and somehow manage to sleep, London Ontario would permeate my dreams, and upon awakening the next day, it would still be at the forefront of my consciousness, thereby ruining a second day—it is better not to go to bed, it is better not to sleep, it is better not to think of London Ontario, the town in which I grew up, the town that I abandoned, the town that I loathe—and yet I am *always* thinking of London Ontario, the town where my mother still lives, more or less, on the graceful curving street known as Blackpool Drive. More or less. But the letter wasn't from my mother, the letter was from Robert Crow of 97 Blackpool Drive, the next-door neighbour. My mother lives at 99 Blackpool Drive. She doesn't *actually* live there. To tell the truth, I don't know where she lives. But *legally*, she lives there. I own the house and she legally lives there. In recent years she has not actually lived there. My family, my cousins aunts and uncles, have not told me where she actually lives, and I do not ask. I am curious, and I have suspicions, but I do not ask. I own the house in London Ontario. The bank is not involved with that house. I truly own it. There are some who claim that I do not own it. But I do. I have the papers. And they are clear. My poor brother and I inherited the house from my grandmother. My mother is the life tenant of the house. She has what is known as a *life interest* in the property. This is stipulated in my grandmother's will. It is set down in a codicil. I don't know if they use codicils much now that there are word processors. They probably just stick in the changes and print again. But back then, in 1961, it would have meant retyping the whole miserable document. Back then a codicil made sense. The codicil states: *My daughter shall have a life interest in my said residential property known as 99 Blackpool Drive.* This sentence made my mother the life tenant when my grandmother died, although my mother does not now occupy the house, and I don't know where she is. My grandmother, in her wisdom, wrote the first version of the will, before the addition of the codicil, with the help of her lawyer. Then she made the mistake of telling my mother about it, she told my mother that she intended to give the property on Blackpool Drive to my brother and me. I remember Grandma's very words: *Now I have taken care of the boys*—meaning my poor brother, now dead, and myself, still alive. She was proud of this will. And she was relieved. My father was dead; my brother, despite unusual ability, had determinedly flunked out of school; I was lazy and sullen. My grandmother was concerned about us. She wanted us to have a stake, a chance. With this will, she had, in her mind, secured our future. She knew from experience that if she put the property in the hands of my mother, it would somehow lead to disaster—things in the hands of my mother have always led to disaster—and Grandma, in her wisdom, acted to avert disaster. But when Grandma, in her wisdom, blabbed about the will, my mother threw herself off the deep end and began the shrieking ruckus that led in the end to the addition of the codicil now pinned to the back of the baby-blue cardboard binder containing the will. My grandmother added the codicil on the advice of my cousin, a truly brilliant guy who was often consulted in family matters, and still is. In this way my mother was appeased. It was only a slight revision. The boys got the property as before *and* my mother got a life interest in the property. My mother didn't trust her boys to put her up in her old age. So she got it in writing in the codicil that was added twenty-nine years before the letter took a dive through the mail slot and belly-flopped onto the gleaming floorboards of my front hall, the letter from Robert Crow the neighbour living in the house next to my house in London Ontario, the house legally occupied by my mother. I had met Robert Crow once. I vaguely remembered him as a decent fellow. And yet for some reason, he now felt compelled to send me a letter. It shows how wrong first impressions can be, I reflected. He goes to the trouble of finding my address in Vancouver and my postal code and writes me a letter that has already ruined my day. This is not the act of a decent person, I reflected. Casual acquaintances do not do such things, I reflected. I did not open the letter. I did of course open the letter. But I did not open it immediately. The letter that had burst through the slit in my door. I was in no hurry to open it. I left it on the floor where it had fallen, walked to the kitchen, plugged in my telephone and dialled Ariadne in Arizona. You should have gone with Ariadne, I said to myself, then you would not have seen the letter as it fell through the air and plopped down on the floor like some dead bird. You could have gone with her to the desert, I said to myself. You could have had a sexual experience in the desert. Ariadne might have gone along with something like that. But you stayed in Vancouver, you stayed to work, and now you find you are too lazy to work. Today you don't work because of the letter, tomorrow you'll find a new excuse. You have always been too lazy, I said to myself. You haven't changed. You think you have, and in a sense you have, but in essence you have not. This meditation was cut short by a man's voice on the telephone. It was Ariadne's father in Arizona. He said that Ariadne had gone to see the rodeo. Or maybe, he said, she had gone to see the big cats at the Wild Kingdom in the desert. One or the other, he said, but probably not both. He asked me how things were. I said fine. It was the first lie of the day. My day was already ruined by the letter that had crash-landed in the front hall, the letter from London Ontario. And now to compound matters, I was lying. It disgusts me to lie. I am confused when I lie. I am paralyzed when I lie. I am strangled by my lies. I often lie. When I am asked the most simple question, such as that asked by Ariadne's father in Arizona, I lie. My first impulse is to lie. I learned this as a child. My mother taught me this lesson. I don't recall her ever telling the truth about anything. I assumed this was the natural and proper way to behave. Once in kindergarten I lied to the teacher about my leggings. It was winter and I wore my little grey wool leggings over my corduroy trousers. The rule was clear: you took your leggings off in the classroom if you had your trousers underneath; on the other hand, if you didn't have your trousers underneath, you kept your leggings on. The teacher stared at my leggings and told me to take them off. I told her I didn't have my trousers underneath. She told me I was a liar. She dragged me to the front of the class and pulled down my leggings and revealed my brown corduroy trousers, which were indeed underneath my leggings, and she told me again that I was a liar. She had me figured out. Liar, she repeated, liar, liar, liar, she chanted as I sat on the floor and struggled to pull the leggings over my shoes. I should add that I had always found taking off my leggings a difficult and boring chore, that even in kindergarten I was lazy, that I had thought the lie would save me from the effort of peeling off my leggings. *Lazy and a liar.* How early in life we show our true colours. I had lied about my trousers and I paid for it with my humiliation before my classmates. I lied about it because I assumed it was the appropriate thing for me to do. I had learned to lie from the very beginning. I have since learned what it is to tell the truth. As a child I of course experimented with the truth, telling my mother where I had really gone after school, telling her that I spent my allowance on firecrackers or baseball cards, telling my mother how I really felt about school, friends, family and life. Her reaction to these experiments proved conclusively

that a lie was preferable to the truth. My mother screamed at me
for saying things like that to her. How could I possibly, she
screamed, say things like that. She had no interest in the truth.
I admire her consistency in this, the way she lied to everyone, the
psychiatrists, the lawyers, the tax collectors, the door-to-door
salesmen, the milkman, the meter reader, the cleaning lady, her
brothers sisters parents and children. My mother had lies enough
for all. And I'm sure that wherever she is now, and I don't know
where that is, she is inventing new lies. At this very moment she
is in all probability lying to someone. I learned to lie from her.
I don't know where she learned to lie. Not from *her* mother.
Grandma was not a liar. She was a notorious teller of the truth.
If only she had been a liar, she could have lied to my mother
about the will and there would have been no ruckus, no codicil,
no life interest and, twenty-nine years later, no letter spurting
through the door to fall towards the molten navel of the earth,
a fall interrupted, unfortunately, by the tongue and groove
flooring in my front hall. I myself have of course told the truth
on occasion. To myself and others. I know how to tell the truth.
But I always have the impulse to lie. I find it difficult to tell the
truth, the lie springs instantly to my lips, yet, despite my natal
inclination, I choke down the lie and cough up the truth. And
many times I have regretted telling the truth. I have wounded
someone with the truth, when to lie would have been the correct
procedure. How did you like my performance of Lady Macbeth?

an actress once asked me. I didn't understand a word of it, I replied. This was the truth. She never spoke to me again. All I needed to say was that it was memorable or provocative or intriguing or stirring. But no, the great liar had to tell the truth and lose a friend. What good was the truth to me that night? And what if I had told Ariadne's father in Arizona the truth? He asks me how things are, and I tell him the truth: that a letter launched by some anonymous person whapped down on the floor and ruined my day because it's from Robert Crow the neighbour in London Ontario, that this letter has, I assume, something to do with my mother, *that I don't even know where my mother is*, nor am I attempting to find out where she is, although I would like to know where she is. What if I said that? What would he think of me then? What would he think of the truthful man who lives with his daughter, the monster who is breaking the Fifth Commandment given to Moses which states that one should *honour one's parents so that thy days may be prolonged, and it may go well with thee, in the land which the Lord thy God giveth thee—* now there's an unveiled threat—and I know one thing: to honour your mother you have to know where she is and I don't— what would he think, the father of Ariadne, a nice guy, a family man? The truth is that he would find it inconceivable, inexplicable that I don't know where my mother is. The truth is he would think I was *lying*. He would think his daughter was living with a liar. And she is. And yet I would be telling him the truth. I do not know where my mother is. And so when I got Ariadne's father on the telephone, I naturally lied to him in order to avoid the deleterious consequences of the truth. I think it was a good move. I routinely lie on the telephone. It's easier somehow on the telephone. I think most people lie on the telephone. This is one of many reasons why I detest the telephone. The ringing of the telephone invariably fills me with horror. This is why I leave it unplugged. My callers have repeatedly advised me to get an answering machine. They say this will solve everything. But I am wary of technological solutions to behavioural problems. If you have an answering machine you have to return the calls. You don't really have to return the calls, they—my callers—tell me. But in truth, you do. It's a lie to say you don't have to return the calls. Why do my callers lie to me all the time? Once you hear the desperate message, which is almost always a lie, on the machine, you are compelled to call back and tell your own lies. And if you resist, if you don't call back, the machine itself lies, it says leave your name and number and I will get back to you, one of the biggest and most popular lies of all time. These machines are instruments fabricated for lying. Human beings are organisms constituted for lying. Put the two together and the truth has but little chance. On the other hand, if you possess no machine, if you receive no message, then you are relieved, at least in this telephonic situation, of the compulsion to lie. Or tell the truth. Unplugging simply improves matters further. *To lie* is a well-known verb, but where is the verb *to truth*? The truth is that the verb *to truth* is not needed, not in this world. There is not enough truth in this world even to justify a verb! Yet my callers resent me for unplugging. They are jealous of my freedom not to lie. Or tell the truth. Why don't they just mind their own business? You're trying to get something done, you're trying to write, you're trying to make love, you're trying to cook a meal, you're trying to read—no wonder the illiteracy rate is ascending exponentially—you're just getting into the funny papers when Braang! The telephone detonates and you must start telling lies again, and so you tell your lies and you close off, and you return to your task, somewhat shaken by your own mendacity, you find your way back into your task, something you truly want to do and BRAANG! It begins again. And the lying goes on. How can I get any work done, I regularly ask myself, when I'm so busy lying on the telephone all the time? And why, one might ask, do my callers call? It's not as if they like me. That's not why they call, my callers, no—they call me because they *want* something from me, because I can do something for them, at least they think I can. I can't, I can't do anything for anybody, I can't even obey the Fifth Commandment. They want me to do something for them. But I can't. And even if I could I wouldn't. I don't have that kind of energy. I can barely get myself through the day, for Christ's sake. They call me and want me to come to their events, their exhibits, their shows, their fundraisers, their bingos, their

rehearsals, their meetings, their birthday parties. I will be there,
I lie. Or I'm booked up, I lie. They call and ask for donations. I'm
broke, I lie. Or, I'll send along a cheque, I lie. They call and say
can we stay with you while we're in Vancouver? It's not possible,
I lie. They call and they call. I lie and I lie. And so to avoid my
callers, ergo, to avoid lying, I unplug. Let my callers come over
and knock on the door if they need me so badly. But no, that does
not occur. That would be too much trouble for my callers. They
would never dream of coming over and knocking. They don't
like me enough to come over and knock and talk right in my face.
And I don't blame them. And so I unplug and nobody knocks on
the door and that's just fine with me. I wouldn't answer the door
anyway. But get a telephone, plug it in, and anybody thinks he
or she has the right to make it go off, anybody at all. Get a phone
and your name is public knowledge. It is published in the
telephone directory. Anyone who knows the alphabet can get at
you. And they do, constantly. Except of course, for my mother,
it would never occur to *her* to call me, to let me know where she
is. No. Or my family. They have telephones. They too could call
me. Many of them are wealthy people who could easily afford a
long distance call. The poorer ones could phone collect. I would
accept the charges. No problem. They have phones, push-
button phones, cordless phones, cellular phones. And they use
them constantly. They are big liars, all of them. All telephone
users are liars. The authorities should consider this when they

tap telephones. The police are always tapping everybody's telephones trying to find out what they're thinking, and the police are hearing nothing but lies because nobody tells the truth on the telephone. The police of this world are getting more and more confused because of the telephone. And if callers don't literally lie on the phone, they nevertheless use the telephone to lie in other ways. Most sexual infidelities, for instance, are arranged on the phone. The furtive lovers get on the phone and make arrangements behind their husband's or wife's back. That's how I got together with Ariadne, and I am grateful to the inventor of the telephone for it. Telephones have their uses. They're not all bad. They come in attractive colours. And of course when you want a pizza it's nice to have a phone. And the truth is that I have never once lied to the pizza man, an individual whom I don't care about in the least. On the other hand, I did lie to Ariadne's father whom I quite like. Perhaps he lied to me as well. He told me that Ariadne had gone to see the rodeo or maybe to the big cats at the Wild Kingdom in the desert. And I believed him. Although it may not have been true. The rest of our conversation was uneventful. I managed not to tell further lies. I said goodbye. I hung up. I thought about unplugging the telephone. But I did not. I reflected that the day was ruined already by the insertion of the letter through the hole in the middle of my front door. My concentration was shattered. Work was now impossible. So I left it plugged in. Give the callers their chance, I thought. The truth is I wanted to be interrupted. I knew that I was going to do nothing today and I wanted to be interrupted while doing it. I wanted to be disturbed, to have a caller ask me for some benevolence that I would not or could not provide, to have a caller rescue me from the letter that had fallen to the floor in the hall, some caller who would take me away. I should have gone with Ariadne to the Arizona desert for sun and sex and shopping, I reflected, but no, I had to stay here in Vancouver in order to see a letter from London Ontario penetrate the door, invade my home, and slap down on the floor of my front hall like a hand spanking a child. No caller is going to rescue you, I said to myself, no caller is going to bother with you, no caller is going to take you to a movie or to some pleasant eatery or to Joe's Cafe for espresso. No. No caller is going to do that. And do you know why no caller is going to do that? I said to myself. They all think you have the phone unplugged and they've given up trying to call! That's why. Nor will they come over, I repeated to myself. They don't want your company. And I can't say that I blame them. They want you to do things for them. But they know by now that you won't. And so they no longer even bother to ask. In the midst of these considerations it occurred to me, suddenly, as I waited for the phone to ring, although I knew it would not because no caller could be bothered calling me anymore, it occurred to me, suddenly, that I could burn the letter without even reading it. Take it to the stove, set it afire, put it in the sink and watch it oxidize. I have done such things before, I have burned unopened letters, letters that I assumed would cause me trouble, pain, or confer an obligation. There was the case some years ago, for example, of a letter sent by one of my more mature students, a nurse by training, in her mid-thirties, married to a respected Vancouver physician, mother of four boys all under eight—a nervous vaguely attractive woman, a stage-struck housewife who had returned to university to study the theatre. Her name was Loretta. She had a new Buick and an agent. Not to mention an answering machine. You can always bet there will be trouble ahead when they come to acting class and they've already got a Buick and an agent. Loretta routinely skipped acting class in order to audition for advertising gigs, usually magazine spreads. She had that anorexic countenance, pale blond and skeletal, which has become popular with housewives in recent decades—not that Loretta was anorexic, far from it—she ate like a pig. I frequently saw her in the corridor outside the studio forcing cheesecake or similar confections into her face—but it didn't register on her body—everything went right through Loretta. More often than not, due to her emaciated appearance, she would get the advertising gig and skip still more classes. On occasion, she would approach me after class, one that she managed to attend, and present me with a magazine or news-paper reproducing her gaunt image; she would show it to me as if such public exposure somehow conferred upon her a *special* theatrical status that entitled her to *special* considerations. I still recall some of these photos: in one she was wet, a monstrous white bath towel shrouding her body; in another she was dry, lying with closed eyes in a field of white flowers; in still another she was naked, on a large bed, kneeling covertly behind a man wearing a partially opened white satin bathrobe, her bony arm draped over his shoulder, her hand reposing on his hairless bronze chest. Things are moving along, Loretta would say to me, don't you think so? My agent wants me to do a film now. When I suggested to her that it would not be unreasonable to attend class periodically and attain at least the fundamentals of her art form, she regarded me with horror and pity. There was no space in her intellectual universe for the concept of acting as an art form. In her opinion, I had missed the point, the point being that you are exposed to the public, in any way possible, and as much as possible, and when you are exposed enough, when your image has been sifted through enough television screens and projected through enough movie projectors and splattered on enough newsprint, *then* you are an actor. I don't blame her for thinking this, many people think this, much of the sad junk that we see on television or in films, which is all most people know, has little to do with the art of acting, the crap that passes for acting is indeed akin to modelling, is indeed about having an image and having an agent and going to auditions and having an answering machine. I doubt she had ever even bothered to go to the theatre where one can actually see real actors going about their work. What would have been the point? Acting was one of the aspects of being an actor that held no interest for Loretta. So, one might ask, what was this wan blond housewife doing in acting class? Once, in point of fact, I asked her precisely this question. She replied that she was learning *a few tricks*, these were her very words, *a few tricks to get her into character*. So much for the art of acting. Of course this answer was not the whole truth, for despite her indifference to the art form, Loretta had her reasons for occasionally coming to class. The truth is that she needed companionship, needed to be around people, needed to be appreciated. The truth is that Loretta was going mad in the suburbs sequestered with her respected physician husband and her four boys under eight and her white Buick. Many come to the theatre for similar reasons—the camaraderie, the ensemble, the approval—and there is typically a place for such people in the theatre. To paraphrase scripture: there are many rooms in the theatre. Loretta wanted a room where she could be liked. And her fellow students did like her, more or less, for she was an attractive person, in a thin sort of way, attractive enough to nail down a middle-aged physician who installed her out in the distant suburbs and bought her a Buick and impregnated her four times in succession. They were trying for a girl, she explained, but after the fourth boy they gave up trying.

Physicians, respected physicians, who have often told me how much they despise nurses, typically marry nurses—such as Loretta—and they methodically have large families, and they are always trying for something with their families, I do not know what—perhaps a team of some kind—although this might prove a laborious undertaking. It would, for example, take nine boys, at minimum, to field a baseball team; on the other hand, a mere six boys would produce a hockey team; and, now that I think of it, you could get away with having only three girls if you opted instead for a backup group like the Raelets. But whatever it was they were trying for, they finally gave up and Loretta was free to take up her career as an actor, free to associate with people other than her physician husband and her four boys all under eight, free to find people that would like her. And the students did indeed like her, more or less, but it was not enough. For Loretta was intent on being liked to excess. She wanted to be at the very centre of the world's affection, she wanted her mere presence to fill the hearts of those around her, she wanted to be special. But there was no one in class with the energy for that kind of thing. There was no one in her life with the energy for that kind of thing. No one liked Loretta that way. Not to excess. Not even her greying respected physician and the four kids under eight. That is the way life goes, I reflected, the thing we want the most is the thing that is most difficult for us to acquire. And when it became clear that she was not liked to excess, she decided to *force* people to like her to excess. She began to throw parties at her home in the distant suburbs, and the students, loyal and generous to a fault, repeatedly dragged themselves out to her house in the distant suburbs, and stuffed themselves with her amusements, as she called them, her jalapeño cheese bites, her Cajun popcorn, her spiced party nuts, her oriental stuffed mushrooms, her miniature frankfurters, her fruit kebabs, her Screwdrivers, Bloody Marys and Black Russians. I too was invited. But I did not go. Instead I learned about these and other amusements from the students who described them in obsessive detail; they described her black refrigerator and her black stove and her black dishwasher and her black housekeeper from the islands who wore a little black uniform. This was in the seventies before people had all that black in their kitchens. Loretta was ahead of her time. It was a death kitchen, said one of the brighter students. The students described as well the silent ageing physician husband who sometimes moved his lips but never uttered a sound and the four boys under eight years of age glazing themselves in the light of the television. The students felt a perverse compulsion to describe to me these jolly evenings in the distant suburbs which began to occur with alarming frequency, evenings that I resolutely refused to attend. The students began to pressure me. They knew that it was important to Loretta that I attend. But I would not attend. I would not journey out to her sordid little soirées. I would not encounter her expansive asphalt driveway, her satanic appliances, her indentured housekeeper, her robo-brats or her mute physician husband. My declination became an issue. Loretta became imperious in her invitations. I was astonished at the intensity of her need. And the truth is, of course, that she needed my presence not only to give me a special opportunity to like her to excess, the real truth is that she had a deeper purpose, a more urgent one, than simply procuring my affection, the real truth is that she required my presence because she wanted me to confirm her life, the life she had carved out for herself in the distant suburbs, she needed me to approve, to affirm, to authenticate, to sanction this life, she needed me to witness it, to make it real for her, she needed all of us to witness it, *the real real truth is that she wanted me to come out there and see all her junk, her property*, the real truth is that Loretta had *an ontological lust for verification*, she needed to be verified out there in the distant suburbs, she needed an audience out there. And who can blame her? But I would not go. I was not interested in attending performances starring Loretta and a supporting cast which included an aphonic physician, four young video addicts, a displaced soul from the islands, and a kitchen by Darth Vader. It was not my kind of show. And the more she pressed me to attend, the more determined I became not to. She would take me aside after class and demand that I come. She would write me cute little invitations. She would phone to remind me. But I would not go. If she wants my approval, I said to myself, she can learn to act. If I attend, if I capitulate, Loretta will never learn to act, I said to myself, she will always find a way to be special and avoid the work of becoming an actor, I said to myself. I felt pure when I said such things to myself, as if it really mattered whether or not this slender blond from the distant suburbs learned to act in a world already overcrowded with actors. I was a purist, a teacher, a guru—I was practically a saint! By the end of the term Loretta was virtually begging me to come. I remained firm. Finally, after classes ended, Loretta sent me a thick letter which sat on my desk for a time. I knew that it contained disturbing revelations about my character and my actions or lack of actions towards her, about my work as a teacher, about my very right to walk on the earth, I knew that it was an act of vengeance, and I avoided opening it. Each morning I sat at my desk and didn't open it. I didn't open it several mornings in a row. Finally, one morning, I took it outside and burned it on the sidewalk. It was a cool morning, and as the letter burned, I squatted down like a good old cowboy at the camp-fire and warmed my hands for a spell. I watched it turn brown, then black, then curl up and shrivel. The envelope peeled away from the contents within, for an instant I saw the word *deserved* as it was pierced by an arrow of flame and obliterated. That one word is all I read of Loretta's letter. Somebody deserved something, somebody was *special*, somebody didn't get what they deserved. Was it me? Or her? I will never know. Not in this world. And yet, I am curious. And if there is an afterlife, I will definitely check to see if God has a copy in the heavenly data bank that I might be permitted to read. And at that point, Loretta, I will give it careful study, I promise. For I think of this letter often. I wonder about it. Judging from the bulk of the envelope, it was a long letter, it represented time and effort, probably more time and effort than she had put into her class work, though not as much as she had put into her deadly little presentations out there in the distant suburbs. And I burned it. My student had finally expressed her true feelings, she had taken the trouble to write something from her heart and I burned it. I would not read it, just as I would not go out there to the distant suburbs and meet her zombie physician, and her four potential serial killers all under eight, and her slave from the Caribbean, about whom little was ever said, and her funeral-parlour kitchen. I burned it and I felt liberated when I burned it. We often believe that we can liberate ourselves through some decisive act—whether it is a petty act such as the burning of the letter, or a momentous act, such as a divorce, a murder, or a major purchase—but we cannot. We act and we believe that we have liberated ourselves in one fell swoop, but we have not. We feel liberated, but we are not liberated. The truth is we are commonly enslaved by those very acts that are intended to set us free. We get the divorce, for example, we finally break away, and this results in our becoming enslaved in an even more abominable relationship; we murder, for revenge perhaps, or to remove an obstacle from our lives, and we think that all will now be well, but the crime creates new enemies and new obstacles, and suddenly we must murder again or possibly we go to jail, possibly we are executed; we buy the exorbitant product, the product that will change our life, make us independent, happy, but we soon find that it merely enslaves us further, makes us more dependent, more helpless than before, more miserable. We think we can cut the Gordian knot, and all will be well for ever and ever, but after we cut it, we spend the rest of our life desperately trying to tie it together again. On the other hand, some acts do have their intended results: my divorce, for example, the second, functioned as intended, it liberated me from an odious marriage, which I will not describe at this time, and as a result I now live with Ariadne, a woman I adore. This is, unhappily, a rare exception. Some years after I burned the letter, Ariadne ran into Loretta and subsequently reported to me that Loretta had undergone surgery for breast cancer. After the surgery, Loretta told Ariadne, she was even thinner, and got even more work modelling. I'm just glad it wasn't my face, she said to Ariadne. In thinking back, I remember Loretta with fondness. In thinking back, I like Loretta. I admire her tenacity and ambition. I do not remember myself with equal fondness. It would have been nothing for me to go out there to the distant suburbs as she wanted me to do, a minor capitulation. I would do it now without hesitation. Of course now no one invites me anywhere.

And I don't blame them. In thinking back, I have nothing but contempt for my own actions, in particular the act of burning the letter, the mere memory of it incapacitates me for hours. And I have many such incidents in my past. And I think of them chronically. It would have been nothing for me to read her letter, to understand what happened from her point of view. But I was too cowardly to face the possibility that Loretta would tell me something about myself that I did not want to hear. Since then, of course, I have heard *everything* about myself that I did not want to hear. Many many times. If Loretta sent me that letter now I would read it, I reflected, as I lingered by the phone avoiding the letter that had shot through the mail slot of my front door and skidded to a stop on the polished pine floor of my front hall, the letter that had ruined my day, the letter from London Ontario. And I wanted, of course, to burn this letter, too, I had an overwhelming urge to burn this letter. But I knew that I would not. I knew that I would open it and that I would read it and that I would regret reading it. I knew that I would not learn anything horrifying about myself that I did not already know, but that I would regret reading it nevertheless. And knowing this, I went to the front hall and picked up the letter, a flimsy letter, almost weightless, almost floating on the palm of my hand. The stamp bore a photograph of the Queen of England, who in turn bore an uncanny resemblance to my mother, the same forced smile, the same maniacal look in her eyes as if she might throw a screaming fit at any moment—even the dress looked familiar, a white brocade with little white flowers embroidered along the neckline—only the diamond-studded crown distinguished this woman, the Queen of England, from my mother, at least in my mind, and I did not know where either of them was currently, nor was anyone going to tell me. I lifted this practically weightless letter from the floor in the front hall and carried it to the kitchen table. I took a butcher knife out of a drawer and prepared to cut into the envelope. At that moment the phone rang. Some caller wants something from me, I sighed to myself. I let it ring nine times. I picked up. There was no one on. My callers are not patient people, I reflected. My callers are in a hurry. If you are not hovering by the phone when they call, if you are not poised to pounce, if you do not jerk into action at the bell like some Pavlovian trainee, if you do not drop everything and sprint for the phone, even if you are in the bath, or otherwise engaged, if you do not get there lickety-split, my callers close off, moving on, no doubt, to other calls. Of course there are occasional callers who hold and wait through as many as twenty rings. Those are the real nuts. When the phone rings twenty times *you must never never pick it up*. Never. It can only be trouble, it can only be a caller who is desperate, psychotic or bored, it can only be some maniac, some malcontent, some bushwhacker scouring the telephone directory for a victim foolish enough to pick up after twenty rings, it can only be some morbid wretch capable of any sort of telephonic abomination. Now if a caller rings nine times, as my previous caller had, that caller is civilized, impatient but civilized, the kind of caller one would like to be with on the telephone. Too bad I missed that caller, I said to myself, as I returned to the letter from London Ontario which had, with a sharp report, terminated its transcontinental trek on the solid burnished floor of the foyer. Once again, I noted that it was from Robert Crow the neighbour who lives at 97 Blackpool Drive, whom I once had met briefly, whose genial behaviour had deceived me into thinking that he was a decent type, who had made use of the postal service to ruin my day, possibly my week, possibly more. I stabbed the envelope with my knife, slashed it open and withdrew its contents through the incision. As I unfolded the single sheet of white paper I became aware of a nauseous sensation in my solar plexus. This was not unfamiliar. I am frequently disgusted by my mail. How different from the old days, I reflected, when as a child I enjoyed receiving opening and reading my mail, when I had pen pals and a subscription to *Boys' Life*, when my friends would send me cards for my birthday, or Valentine's Day or other important days, those days long ago when I had friends. *Friends always become enemies if you wait long enough*—Giorno, the poet, said that. And he is right. My friends have either become enemies, or have died before they had the chance. Neither group sends me letters. And I don't blame them, I reflected, as I sat at the kitchen table holding the letter in my

hands, the letter from Robert Crow, the vaguely sociable neighbour whom I had met in the late summer during a visit, the
disastrous visit, to London Ontario one year before. I tried to
picture Robert Crow, the putative narrator of the invasive
missive, the Robert Crow who lives next door to the house I had
inherited along with my poor brother, now dead, the house
legally occupied by my mother, now missing, the house in which
I grew up, and left more than thirty years ago, I tried to picture
Mr. Robert Crow—but I could not. The brain cells containing
his image were either secure against all conscious intrusion or
dead. I could only remember an air of boyish congeniality, an
ambience of the easygoing, a feeling that he was young and fair
and understanding, a trifle effeminate perhaps, but not suspiciously effeminate, the kind of clean-living laughing Canadian
boy who joined the army in World War II and got blown apart
by a grenade, the kind of normal white Canadian male who
inherited a little money and got married and settled down and
had a few kids and hoped for a pleasant happily ever after—just
an innocent regular guy who had unfortunately bought a house
next to the house that was legally occupied by my mother and
owned by me. I remembered the impression created by Robert
Crow, but I could not remember Robert Crow. There was
something negative lurking in my memory, something that had
disturbed me about my meeting with Robert Crow, but I could
not remember any details. I have a good memory, but at the time

PROPERTY

I made the acquaintance of Robert Crow, in the late summer, I was in an agitated frame of mind, due to certain things that occurred during my travels through the twisting streets of London Ontario, and in consequence I did not remember him as well as I normally might; and it was, I reflected sitting at my kitchen table in Vancouver holding the letter in my hands, not the first time that I had grown confused during a sojourn in London Ontario, although it was, I hoped, the last. To be brief: back at the beginning of the summer I had gone to London Ontario to explore the possibility of selling my property. That doesn't sound too bad, does it? People sell their property every day. Of course there was the small matter of my mother, the legal occupant of the house, who at that time, last summer, did not live in the house, although at least I knew where she did live, unlike now, but that small matter had been settled. At least in my mind. Unfortunately, as I have discovered in my dealings with my family, sometimes things are settled in my mind, but nowhere else. It certainly had the appearance of being settled: my family, cousins aunts uncles and in-laws, along with certain members of the psychiatric community frequented by my mother, had been urging me for some time to sell my property on Blackpool Drive. My mother would move to a seniors' facility of some kind and all would be well. I had been reluctant to sell because my mother loved her garden, cherished her own peculiar independence, was afraid of old-persons' homes, seniors' apartment buildings, retirement havens and so on—and I don't blame her. But now, I somewhat grudgingly agreed, the time had come to take action. And so at the beginning of the summer I went to London Ontario, a year before Robert Crow's letter toppled to the pine floor, to talk to my mother about selling the property. At that time, I even knew where she was. She was in the London Psychiatric Hospital on Highbury Avenue—the crazy house. She frequently spends time in psychiatric institutions and has since the middle of the century. They did the usual things to her: psychotherapy group therapy drug therapy shock therapy aversion therapy dance therapy whatever therapy or combination of therapies happened to be in fashion that year; and some things worked for a while, but nothing worked permanently. She would go home, have another episode, as they say, and would return to the psychiatric hospital. In the months before the beginning of last summer's London Ontario adventure, a simple-hearted time when I still plugged in my telephone, the campaign to persuade me to sell my property intensified. The respected psychiatrist, Dr. Frisch, an Austrian, stunned me, for example, with a series of 5:00 a.m. calls. He began each call the same way: Oh dear did I wake you? Is the time different out West? Terribly sorry. And then he would urge me to sell my property, the implication being that this was a good idea for medical reasons. I wrote Dr. Frisch a polite letter asking him to explain his medical reasoning to me, and also requesting that he phone after 8:00 a.m. I included a map of Canada which delineated the time zones. He did not write back. And I don't blame him. But at least he never phoned again. I was also informed by my cousin, a truly brilliant guy, the financial doyen of the family, a wise and reliable entrepreneur, a Christian businessman who dealt in jewels and real-estate and sound advice, that it was time to sell my property. Everyone, with the possible exception of my mother, wanted me to sell my property. Finally, at the beginning of the summer, I flew east to London Ontario, entered the unending corridors of the psychiatric hospital, and asked my mother what she thought about selling the property. She told me to stop smiling, that there was nothing to smile about. She hated my smile she said. I stopped smiling. I asked her again about the property. She told me the police were going to arrest her because she had killed a cat. She was preoccupied with this cat murder. She came back to it again and again. She was going to prison, she said, because of what she had done to this cat. I thought, based on past experience, that she was lying about this cat killing, this felicide, and she was, and yet as I discovered later, she was not, not entirely. I asked her again about the property. She said she thought it was a good idea to sell. She said that she could no longer keep the house up. Get rid of it, she said. So at last I had her permission to sell my property. And it was the perfect time to do it; not only were prices at an all-time high, but it so happened, coincidentally, that last summer I was flying from Vancouver every other weekend in order to attend the Collaborative Vision, a series of workshops for television writers at the CBC in Toronto, just a few hours up the road from London Ontario. It was, I reasoned, a favourable and convenient time for action, decisive action. After each three-day session I would rent a car, drive to London Ontario, stay over at my brilliant cousin's house in the distant suburbs, where I was always welcome, and lay the groundwork for the sale of my property. My dream was simple: I would sell the property on Blackpool Drive, give a chunk of the proceeds directly to my mother, use the remainder to pay off the mortgage on my property in Vancouver, and use the savings on the mortgage to pay my mother a decent monthly salary. Instead of paying the bank every month, I would pay my mother. I would just as soon pay mother as the bank, I told my brilliant cousin. He chuckled at that. That was my dream. Simple as that. I liked it. The family liked my dream too, so they said. My brilliant cousin liked my dream, so he said. I was relieved. It would mean that I could take care of my mother for the rest of her life. It would mean that she would have a reasonable income for the rest of her life. My dream was clean. It was rational. It was easy. It was impossible. I forgot, momentarily and tragically, a fundamental maxim of life in my family: nothing to do with my mother is easy, nothing. *By the way*, in order to sell the property, my brilliant cousin told me—the same cousin who twenty-nine

years before advised my grandmother to add the codicil now
pinned to the back of the baby-blue cardboard binder of my
grandmother's will, the codicil that gave my mother a life
interest in my property on Blackpool Drive, the property I
inherited with my poor dead brother, the one adjacent to the
property owned by Robert Crow, the neighbour whose genial
appearance is lost in the mists of time, the friendly Robert Crow
who wrote the letter that had come through my mail slot, the
letter that I was now holding in my hands as I sat at the kitchen
table of my house in Vancouver, primarily owned by the bank—
in order to sell the property—the one in London Ontario, that
is, which I more or less own free and clear—two things need to
be accomplished: *first*, said my brilliant cousin, you need to get
your mother to sign a power of attorney; *second*, you need to clean
the place up a little to make it saleable. My brilliant and wise
cousin directed me to a lawyer who was good with old people,
and I arranged to go out to the London Psychiatric Hospital with
this attorney and get my mother to sign the power of attorney.
How I admired my brilliant and wise cousin, twenty years my
senior, who knew about real estate and powers of attorney and
money, who had spent his adult life in the real world buying
and selling and getting rich. I did not, however, admire him
without limitation. I remembered that in the sixties, a few years
after my grandmother wrote her will, he had staunchly supported the U.S. action in Vietnam, and even subscribed to the

domino theory, a comical world view that had virtually nothing
to do with the game of dominoes and even less to do with reality.
That had bothered me, a brilliant guy like that, but what the
heck, he's entitled to his opinion, right? We argued about it.
I also remembered arguing with him back then because he
vehemently opposed political action intended to protect the
environment, he considered such action oppressive to progress
and ominously undemocratic, he said they can take care of the
environment later. I found his point of view disagreeable. Of
course with the populace now embracing the ecological movement with virtually fascistic fervour, with industries hysterically
pushing products purported to enhance, even save, the eco-
system—the same industries that turned the world to shit in the
first place, with movie stars reverently separating their bottles,
cans and paper products on camera, with the children of our
nation practically turning in their own parents for littering, with
the mass media—the same mass media that for decades didn't
even notice there was a problem—blaming the rank and file of
my generation, blaming me, for poisoning the future, as if I
somehow did it by teaching theatre, with all this repulsive
enthusiasm and hypocrisy, I sometimes think my brilliant cousin
might have had a point back then. Of course these days he's
into the ecological movement. These days it makes good financial sense to save the planet, he says. There's no bottom line,
when there's no planet, he jokes. My brilliant cousin scored

sensational grades when he went to school. He wrote perfect exams. In university he was a legend. He was even in *Time* magazine. He was one of the few guys, they said, who understood the theory of relativity. He went off to Princeton for a doctorate, married a girl from Bryn Mawr and did some flashy research on black holes. He showed promise. But in the end he did not realize that promise. My grandmother, in her wisdom, pleaded with him to stick with the sciences, to make a contribution. Instead he returned to the convoluted streets of London Ontario where he had inherited some property. He sold that property and founded a chain of jewellery stores which proved lucrative. He got into stocks and bonds and real-estate. He went into business for himself. He preferred to be independent, to do things his own way. And who can blame him? And when he went into business for himself, my grandmother was bitterly disappointed in him, and she wrote him off, although he never figured this out, despite his brilliance. And who can blame her? She knew that he was the one person the family had produced who was capable of doing something of genuine significance in the world, something that might make a difference, and when he turned away from that she could not forgive him. This brilliant cousin had four wonderful children, all girls, and those girls found their way out of town, out of London Ontario, as soon as they were old enough, putting ample distance between themselves and their brilliant father, but he's never figured this out either, why they left so precipitately, and he never will, because finally there comes a point when you're too brilliant to figure out anything. When I was a kid, two or three decades back, this brilliant cousin took me camping and taught me how to sail and gave me tips on the stock market, tips that eventually paid my tuition in university. He was a perfect being, this brilliant cousin. When my mother got into legal trouble, financial trouble, psychiatric trouble, he was there to help out. He was generous with his time and energy, this brilliant cousin. He was a good guy. How I admired and idolized my brilliant cousin with his quick mind and easygoing ways. And so, last summer, when he told me how straightforward it was to sell the property, when he sanctioned the dream that would enable me to support my mother and pay off my property in Vancouver, I knew it was a good dream. I believed him. I had no reason not to believe. That he was reputed to be a shrewd guy in a business deal, a tough customer, did not concern me. This wasn't, after all, a business deal, this wasn't the world of commerce, this was family. *By the way*, said my brilliant cousin, let's you and I share the power of attorney. Then when you're out there in Vancouver, I'll be in a position to expedite matters here in London. That sounded like a sensible plan to me. I opted for it. I was grateful. Surprised. Even flattered. The truth is, I knew that he was tired of my mother and her problems which had gone on for decades; in point of fact, I knew that he was fed up with my mother, and still he offered to share the power of attorney.

What a guy! What a great and brilliant guy! And when my mother signed the power of attorney, which she did with surprisingly little hesitation, she stated that she was delighted by the inclusion of my brilliant cousin's name on the document. Things were moving along, I reflected. The other matter that had to be taken care of, according to my brilliant and clever cousin, was to clean up the house and make it saleable. No problem, I thought—although, in truth, I had not seen the house for some time. I suspected, of course, that the house, my house, needed a bit of work, and so I went over to the winding street called Blackpool Drive, in the rather desirable neighbourhood known as Old South, to size up the job. I pushed open the front door and entered the topography of my mother's imagination—mounds of newspaper, hillocks of junk mail, drifts of soiled rags and swellings of clothing all combining to obscure the floor of the front hall. I beat a path through to the kitchen where I discovered walls covered with mysterious maps and cryptic messages written in pen pencil crayon and lipstick, where unwashed dishes glasses and cups lay heaped in and around the sink, where black and brown scorch marks scarred the grimy white vinyl floor, site of some ancient battle, where every knob on every cupboard was missing, where cat shit and cat food lay putrified in every corner, where the refrigerator still contained vegetables and bottles of milk and fruit juice that had been stashed there in biblical times, where a profusion of crud-covered knives forks and spoons and filthy plastic containers fossilized on the counters and the shelves and in the drawers, where the electric stove had somehow been dismantled so that it resembled a Rube Goldberg special with elements hanging here and there and the oven door suspended from its hinges at an odd angle, where all the windows were cracked or broken, where the yellow wall-clock was crushed against the wall and hummed pathetically without moving its hands, where the air was rancid, where the dirt and mould covered every item as if it had been spray-painted on, where even the light switches were mutilated—and as I stood there taking in this hideous landscape, I reflected that my mother had never been much of a housekeeper. I continued to explore. The keys on a once magnificent baby grand were fractured and demented. I picked out a melancholic rendition of 'Baa, Baa, Black Sheep.' I went into a bedroom. More clothes rags and newspapers, more dirt, more cat shit, more broken fixtures, smashed furniture, assorted books with pages torn out, a slashed mattress vomiting its innards; add a bathroom coated with excrement; add major holes in the walls; add a basement filled with rotting garbage, soiled bed sheets and old clothes; add more dirt and shit and newspapers. My house was a garbage dump, a sewage tank, a disease. I gagged a few times, reached the back door and escaped. Things weren't too bad, I told myself. My house had once been a beautiful house. It had changed. I had to admit. It had been changed by the legal occupant of the house, who did not presently occupy the house, but resided in the psychiatric hospital on Highbury Avenue. But all in all things weren't too bad, I repeated to myself. I returned to the distant suburbs and said goodbye to my brilliant cousin and his wife. I assured them that on a future visit I would bring Ariadne along and together we would clean up the house and make it saleable. My brilliant cousin smiled like a Buddha. I drove my rentacar back to Toronto, where I was religiously attending the sessions of the Collaborative Vision, the series of workshops in TV writing at the CBC, I went to the airport and took a plane to Vancouver. I was proud of myself, I was going to fix everything, I was going to sell my property in London Ontario, I was going to pay off my property in Vancouver, I was going to give my mother a decent income for the rest of her life, *I was going to do something right.* My dream was going to come true. It all seemed so simple, I reflected, one year later, as I sat in Vancouver at my kitchen table holding the letter from Robert Crow in my hands, the letter that had ruined my day, it all seemed so rational, so sensible, so obedient to the Fifth Commandment, it all seemed so just, so fair. But that's how things go when you think you've got it all figured out: you're so busy putting the final touches to the master plan, you don't even bother to notice that *the familiar world is dissolving around you,* that the ground is vaporizing beneath you—something goes wrong with your alarm systems;

you are flying through the air and you think you're ready to come in for a smooth landing and you lower the wheels and you break through the clouds and you realize suddenly that something is wrong; you are flying through the air and you break though the clouds and you realize that you are lost; you break through the clouds and you realize that *you've never seen those dark mountains before*; you break through the clouds full of confidence but the landing strip isn't there; you break through the clouds and you realize that you're almost out of gas; you are reaching under your seat for the parachute, hoping that you remembered to pack the parachute; you break through the clouds and you find that *you are falling*, one way or another, *you are falling*. I thought I knew where I was when I took my dream back over the dark mountains. But I did not know where I was. I thought I had good directions, but I did not know right from left, I reflected, one year later, sitting at my kitchen table holding the letter that had plummeted to the wooden floor of my front hall, I did not know up from down, I reflected, I did not know in from out. Life is chock-full of surprises, I reflected. You think you're playing baseball, but you're really playing football and you don't figure it out until someone tackles you right at home plate, you don't figure it out until you feel the pain. That's how life goes, I reflected, not to mention metaphors, you head for the promised land, but you wind up in hell. Take the Collaborative Vision, my workshop in TV writing with the CBC: I thought I knew what

that was about, because they told me what it was about, but I
didn't know what it was about; they knew what it was about, and
they said what it was about, but what they *said* it was about, was
not what it was about. What they *said* it was about and what it
was about were entirely different things. I didn't realize this for
a while. They said they wanted new writers, they wanted fresh
blood, they wanted new ideas, they wanted to shake things up,
they wanted me. They chose only fifteen writers from across the
country. I was honoured. I didn't have a big track record. A
novel, a few plays, a short story or two, one letter to the editor.
I was surprised. Not that surprised, however. For the truth is a
friend of mine was on the selection committee, a fact which
probably increased my chance of being selected. And this didn't
bother me. For in showbiz, a friend is *always* on the selection
committee. That is showbiz. That is life. Without a friend in the
right place, showbiz is no biz. The CBC flew me into Toronto
and gave me a room in the Delta Inn and a per diem and they
taught me TV. Famous TV guys from around the world came in
and taught me. Producers and story editors and buyers and sellers
and directors and execs and even writers. Beaver Winslow, a
producer from the popular horror series *Scary Dinner Party*, was
the very first teacher. Beaver came in and showed us an episode
that, he bragged, he had been forced to rewrite in twelve hours
because some retarded hack, his phrase, had failed to deliver a
decent script. The episode, a tale about a food processor that

takes over the minds of housewives, turning them into savage murderers, was the most shoddy and cynical dreck that I had seen in some time. During the viewing, everyone in the room looked miserable. Except Beaver. Beaver beamed. Beaver was proud of it. Beaver was a pro. Beaver let it be known that he hated it when a writer phoned him up and bothered him about this line or that scene. The writer does the first draft, said Beaver. I tell him what to fix. Then he does the second draft. Then I take the script and I tell the writer to shove off. His work is over. I don't ever want to hear from him again, said Beaver. Beaver said that he hated a writer who objected to having his material rewritten. Beaver said he would never allow a writer to be present on the set of an actual shoot. A writer on the set can only cause trouble and disturb the creative people, he said. Beaver said that a writer who causes trouble would not be around the biz for long. Beaver said that the main thing the writer had to do was to make sure that the viewer stayed there in front of the tube, the main thing, he elaborated, was to make sure the viewer stayed in front of the tube *right through the commercials*. Beaver went on to say that the main thing to do was to kiss his ass. Television is a business, he said, and the main business of the writer is to kiss my ass. He didn't really say this. But he did. TV is a business, he repeated. TV is fast. There is no time to write. It's gotta be good, it's gotta be fast, it's gotta have three acts. It's gotta be twenty-two minutes long. It should make sense. The rest belongs to the sponsor. That's the formula. A half hour is twenty-two minutes long. The act-breaks are the main thing. The commercials. You hook the audience with your story just before the act-breaks. You gotta keep the audience in their seats through the act-breaks, he repeated. You are not a writer, you are a technician, he related, a technician who controls the activities of the viewer during the act-breaks. TV writers, the real pros, never watch the shows they write, he continued, it's too embarrassing. Never watch the shows you write! he commanded. Actually, he chuckled, you probably wouldn't recognize them anyway. Scary Beaver described how he had been testing people with electrodes. When the interest meter goes down, he said, I cut the scene. I stick in some action, a chase or something. What about the new ideas? I interrupted. What about shaking things up? What about fresh blood? That's why we're here in this workshop right? The other writers looked at me as if I had released a noxious fart. The truth is they didn't look at me at all. I looked at them. They gazed into their coffee. And, in retrospect, I don't blame them. Party-animal Beaver ignored my questions, gave me a you'll never work in this industry again smirk and went on with his lecture. I had a suspicion at that point about the true nature of the Collaborative Vision. But it passed. After all, I reasoned, the CBC had spent $500,000 to organize the Collaborative Vision and bring in all these famous TV guys from around the world, not to mention me and my fellow writers, the writers who, as the organizers of the Collaborative Vision were fond of saying, were going to virtually transform the face of television as we know it today; surely, I reasoned, the CBC, the national television network of our country, the communication lifeline of Canada, wouldn't spend half a million taxpayer dollars, in these hard times, the same CBC that was purportedly being bled dry by a hostile government, the same CBC that was being murdered in the ratings by the American networks, the private networks, the public network, the sports network, the feature-film network, the rock-video network, the home-shopping network, the Christian network, the porn network, the Christian-porn network, by almost anybody, in fact, who knew how to plug in a video camera; surely, I reasoned, the CBC wouldn't spend a cool $500,000 to give fifteen handpicked writers, the cream of the crop, as they kept telling us, a very special élite group, as they kept repeating, the hope of the future, as they were enamoured of saying; surely, I reasoned, they wouldn't blow all that cash just to let us know that our job as writers was to kiss Beaver Winslow's ass. And, I reflected as I sat at my kitchen table, one year later, holding the letter from Robert Crow, my enchanting neighbour in London Ontario, I was right. Sort of. It was not that simple. There were other reasons that the CBC had lavished half a million dollars on the Collaborative Vision, far more money, in all probability, than any of the participating writers would make from writing in an entire lifetime—intricate impenetrable reasons of power and politics and territory and property—not straightforward reasons, such as the claim that they needed new writers or the looming presence of Beaver Winslow's ass. Nothing in this world is simple, I reflected. And yet, I keep searching for the simple. The hope, the longing, the quest for the holy simple. That was my mistake last year, I reflected. That has always been my mistake, I reflected. I constantly remind myself that nothing is simple, and then I go out looking for something simple. I thought last year that I could sell my property in London Ontario and buy my property in Vancouver and give my mother a nice income for the rest of her life. I thought that the holy simple was in my hands, the hands that were now holding the letter that had entered my house through the slot and ruined my day. *Everybody wants it simple*, I reflected. I thought I would just sell the property and escape from London Ontario with a clear conscience. I thought I would clean up the house and sell it and that would be that. I thought that I would phone my mother and visit her and send her money every month and take care of her. Simple. And late in the summer, harbouring such thoughts, I drove my rentacar out of Toronto and into the circuitous streets of London Ontario, with my power of attorney in hand, with Ariadne in hand, with my hopes in hand, to begin the big clean-up, the final three-week onslaught, the cure. First we took a look at the house on Blackpool Drive. It had not changed. It was still a shithole. Ariadne was stunned. Next we went over to the house of my

brilliant cousin and his wife in the distant suburbs. My brilliant
cousin insisted that we stay with them. And we agreed. My
brilliant cousin liked the company. He wanted someone to talk
to. He loves to talk. He is a great talker. He leaned back in his
La-Z-Boy and spoke about his real-estate deals, about how he
had finessed business rivals by bluffing, by pretending to be
interested in one parcel of land when he was in fact interested
in another, about the techniques of setting a trap for your
opponents and closing that trap so gently that your opponents
take weeks and sometimes even years to realize that they've been
had. You create diversions, he said, you wear them out by arguing
about trivial details, you soften them up with complications, you
mystify them until they lose their sense of direction and aim-
lessly turn this way and that, you exhaust them, you confuse
them, you break them down, until, finally, scarcely conscious,
they wander into the trap and, as it softly shuts around them,
they are too stupefied to even notice. And timing is everything,
he said, timing is everything. He was brilliant. He brought out
his little display cases and showed us his precious stones, his
diamonds, his sapphires, his opals and other jewels in his
possession, row upon shimmering row against black velvet. He
regretted not having any bloodstones to show us. Bloodstones,
he said, are almost impossible to get. He leaned back in his La-
Z-Boy and informed me there was some problem with the
Humane Society about a cat. *By the way*, he said, there is some

problem about a cat associated with your mother, some cat in a cat hotel, he said, some cat that was running up a monstrous tab at a cat hotel. We all laughed about that one. Crazy things happen around your mother, he said, that's for sure. And we all laughed. He leaned back in his La-Z-Boy and told us about the economy. About the ebb and flow of capital. When he leaned back in his La-Z-Boy it all crystallized, the world made sense, it was a world of opportunities, investments, trends, tendencies. The economic consequences of world events. My brilliant cousin was a financial eagle flying above it all, analysing, waiting for his chance. His wife went to bed. He leaned back in his La-Z-Boy and kept on talking. I asked him about gold and silver. He answered my questions in astonishing detail. He described how the Hunt brothers from Texas had once tried to corner the world silver market; he narrated the whole labyrinthine story from beginning to end, masterfully negotiating every twist and turn leading to the startling downfall of the Hunt boys. I was mesmerized. I sat on the edge of my seat. He leaned back in his La-Z-Boy. I shook my head at the scope of his knowledge, at the penetration of his judgements, at his sheer brilliance. Later, in bed, I said to Ariadne: My cousin, a brilliant guy. He's a very good storyteller, Ariadne replied. In the morning Ariadne drove me through the windings and turnings of London Ontario to the twisted street known as Blackpool Drive where we began cleaning my house, the house legally occupied by my mother.

And one year later, at my kitchen table in Vancouver, holding
the letter from the neighbour, Robert Crow, in my hands, the
letter that entered my house and ruined my day, I attempted to
recall what had happened during those three weeks of cleaning
up, but in my memory there was only a dismal whirl—papers and
dirt and shit and trucks and a real-estate agent and garbage bags
and trips to the lawyer and a hotel room and garbage dumps
and spent tears and unspent tears and visits to the London
Psychiatric Hospital and my mother, brittle and small, sitting in
her chair—a dismal spinning agglomeration of detail and
event without chronology, order, or shape, without beginning,
without end—nothing but middle, nothing but muddle, nothing but misery. My brilliant cousin, I reflected, could handily
remember every detail of the Hunts' sociopathic attempt to get
a stranglehold on the silver market, an event that had occurred
more than a decade before, an event he had not participated
in; but I could not remember those three weeks in London
Ontario, which I had indeed, to the best of my knowledge,
participated in. With a mind like his, I reflected, it was no
wonder he could outmanoeuvre an opponent in a business deal,
a feint here, a phrase there, a deke or two—that's how it is with
business, I reflected, that's the way business is done, you have to
be sharp, like a knife, you can't miss a trick. It's just like life. And
life, for my brilliant cousin, is business, and business, for my
brilliant cousin, is life. And business, let's face it folks, is right

at the centre of things, business is what put this country where it is today. And what is the business of business? Wrong. It is not about making money. The cult of the bottom line is only a symptom of the disease. *The true business of business is murder.* If people could just get this into their heads, that the business of business is murder, then we could all lean back in our La-Z-Boys and really get a handle on the miserable blood bath taken by people all over the world in the twentieth century, the rivers of blood leaking out through bullet wounds and shrapnel wounds and whatever wounds you get when a smart bomb lands on dumb you, we could lean back in our La-Z-Boys and relax as arms legs bones and minds are broken in torture chambers around the world. The business of America, a politician once said, is business. He meant murder. And it's the same here in Canada, a businesslike country that in the sixties and seventies just happened to be the world's largest per capita war exporter— quietly enriching itself from the destruction of Vietnam, while publicly deploring American brutality. It's the same pretty well everywhere. Riding our La-Z-Boys into the slaughter. If Ariadne were here, I reflected holding the letter that had ruined my day, she would help me bring historical order to that grim mazy time in London Ontario, but Ariadne was in Arizona, at the rodeo or at the Wild Kingdom in the desert with the big cats. If only Ariadne were here, I thought again and again. But she was not. *Dear M*—, the letter began. I chose to ignore, for the time being,

the aggravating informality of this salutation, its unearned
familiarity, the impertinent use of the praenomen, I chose to
ignore the fact that I am hardly *Dear M—* to Robert Crow, that
I am not dear to him, that I am not some good old pal, as this
intimate opening phrase insinuates, no, that is not the nature of
our relationship, and in fact we have only met once, briefly, a
meeting which is no clearer in my memory than a cloud I may
have once studied in the summer sky or a trip I may have once
made to a fast-food outlet. If we are such pals good buddy Bobby,
why didn't you write sooner? I should rip this letter into pieces,
I said to myself, crumpling it in my hands. I chose, however, not
to be provoked by the affable Bob Crow's insolent overture, I
chose to restrain myself, for the time being, to concentrate on
reading the opening sentence in the body of the text proper. I
smoothed the letter out on the kitchen table and continued. *I am
the next-door neighbour to your mother's property.* Stop right there,
Bob! You think you live next to my mother's property. But you
do not. It is not my mother's property. My mother has no
property. It is my property! She is the legal occupant of my
property. It says so in the codicil pinned to the back of the baby-
blue cardboard folder containing the will. I'll show it to you
when we have our next tête-à-tête. Bob, you poor guy, do you
realize that you don't even know where you live, that you are lost
in London Ontario? What if you invited someone over to your
place for smart drinks, and you told them that you lived next

door to my mother's property? Your guests might never make it to your house, they would go to city hall to search Mom's title and it would not be there and they would miss the whole party. Bob, you did all the research on my name and address and my postal code, but you failed to go the last mile. My delightful relations, who undoubtedly assisted you with your fact-finding mission, misled you. They don't like to think of the house next to yours as my property. They feel that my grandmother made a mistake, a slip of the pen so to speak, when she composed her will. So they allowed you to think that you live next to my mother's property. Like many people in London Ontario, you are lost and you do not even know it. And who can blame you? People smarter than you, Bob, have gotten lost in London Ontario. My brilliant cousin got lost in London Ontario. My poor dead brother lost his way, not to mention his life, in London Ontario. Many of my friends got lost in London Ontario. My mother is currently lost in London Ontario. I still get lost in London Ontario. When I cross the city limits and enter the serpentine thoroughfares of London Ontario I feel my inner compass whirling. The only thing one should do in London Ontario, a friend once told me, is leave. He did not take his own advice. That friend is now dead. He got lost in London Ontario. I, on the other hand, took his advice. And I am grateful. You could take his advice too, Bob, you could get out. It's not too late. But perhaps you're too busy with your correspondence.

Something is going wrong in the brain of London Ontario. There is something lurking within the gnarled heart of London Ontario that takes the liveliest part of a person and turns it into the deadliest, something in those complacent twisting avenues that makes a person smug and mean and trivial, something embedded deep within the very molecular structure of London Ontario that pervades a person and crushes the spirit. That's how it is with these provincial towns, these little fiefdoms of money, snobbery, fear and good taste, I reflected, as I paused in my reading of the letter that had entered my house through the mail slot. And many spend their whole lives in London Ontario. They are born there and they are buried there. It is as if they have never been. They went to school, they shopped regularly, and they died. Some of the most talented people I have ever known got lost in London Ontario—painters, writers, musicians. They simply could not follow their star. They could not even see it. The self-righteous atmosphere of London Ontario blinded them, suffocated them, poisoned them. Some of these people were suicides, others work as bank tellers or manage convenience stores or teach in career academies, some stack empties at the Labatt's factory. A suspiciously large number work or reside in mental hospitals. There are a lot of crazy people in London Ontario. London Ontario makes them crazy. It made my mother crazy. She had to lie about everything to survive in London Ontario. She was afraid to be herself in London Ontario. And now she has lost herself in London Ontario. I do not know where. People lose selves in London Ontario. People lose everything in London Ontario. And now that I think of it, people even lose their balance in London Ontario. People fall down in London Ontario. Literally. My father, a respected physician, eye ear nose and throat, once told me that there are more diseases of the inner ear, baffling afflictions involving fluids that lose their way among the intorted channels of the semi-circular canals, in London Ontario per capita than anywhere in Canada, diseases leading to vertigo and loss of orientation. It is a beautiful city, London Ontario, with maple trees and parks and fine old houses and a theatre and a university with a terrific business school. The students fight with one another to get into that business school. They want to study murder. No one says that of course, but I suspect most of them know it somewhere in their hard little hearts. And so every year the university turns out hundreds and hundreds of greedy little assassins, killers who have never seen a play, or read a poem, or studied a philosopher, or even perused a volume of history. They cram themselves with nothing but marketing sciences, management sciences, accounting sciences, administration sciences, decision-making sciences. And then these scientists go to work in London Ontario. And who can blame them? There is room for such scientists in London Ontario. They set the cultural and intellectual tone in London Ontario. Fortunately, the rest of the country is far more enlightened, and would never let things be run by a group of bozos who cultivate ignorance as a virtue and believe that greed, self-interest and mendacity are admirable and necessary traits, I reflected. On the other hand, I reflected, when all is said and done, London Ontario isn't really such a bad place, it's quiet at night, it's possible to walk through the sinuous streets without getting mugged, it has a minor league baseball team, a reasonable bookstore, majestic trees, enchanting gardens, pleasant parks, a charming public library, a plethora of psychiatric hospitals and many beautiful churches. Everybody says it's a terrific place to raise a family. I even heard my mother say this once, years ago. The memory of that utterance makes me shudder. This is a woman whose approach to raising a family was lethal. In point of fact, I ran away from home at the age of twelve because *I knew that I was dying in my mother's house.* My hard-working father, a respected physician, had already died in my mother's house. My poor brother would only last a few more years before his fatal 'accident.' And I knew that I too was dying, that if I stayed I only had a few more years left. I doubt I ever said to myself, you are dying in your mother's house, and yet I knew I was. And so at the age of twelve, I made a run for it. I saved my own life at the age of twelve. Now, in retrospect, I realize that my mother was in the forefront of a new era in parenting, that she was a pioneer, so to speak, a member of the avant-garde, anticipating numerous late-century trends. I realize now, in retrospect, thirty-four years later, with the teen suicide rate swelling exponentially, with psychotic and abused kids crammed into hospitals and halfway houses, with pre-pubescent dope addicts falling down stoned in school yards at recess, that her parenting methods have finally been embraced by moms and dads everywhere. And, like mother like son, I was also ahead of my time, I was a new kind of child, a new kind of casualty; for in those days, in the early fifties, twelve-year-olds did not run away from home, not for keeps, not in London Ontario. Of course in the late century it is not unusual for kids to run away from home. Many have no other choice. *Run and live. Remain and die.* The streets are full of these survivors, these casualties. They become dope addicts and prostitutes. Their customers, entrepeneurial types, cruise the streets in their vehicles and pick them up and pay them for a quick fuck or blow job in order to relieve the tension and stress of another hard day at work, they talk to their wives and their own children on cellular phones while the casualties are sucking them dry in parking lots and alleys across the nation. Some casualties, of course, learn to run in different ways; I speak, of course, of the orphans who stayed at home. I have such orphans in my acting classes. The theatre attracts them. They are looking for their family in the theatre. The family they could never find at home. It is a rare acting student who is not, in one way or another, an orphan, who is not, in one way or another, an abused person. Over the long run, as it is called, the long and tortuous run through childhood and adolescence, they have been sexually molested, beaten, brainwashed, and neglected. I tell people about this, but no one wants to hear it. My listeners just stare at me, or change the subject. And I don't blame them. When Freud began to hear tale after tale of sexual abuse from patients, he attributed these *fantasies* to hysteria. I can understand why. Even he couldn't take the truth. And I don't blame him. I found it hard to accept the truth from my students at first. Can you blame me? But over the years their accounts have been persistent and demoralizing and persuasive. To become an actor one must enter the past, the past is the source of the actor's art. Unfortunately, when my students have gone into the past, they have, again and again, made terrible and grotesque discoveries. This is the way I have learned about the parents of my students. This is the way I have learned about the parents of my world. Yes, at first the evidence astonished me, at first I refused to believe the extent of the devastation, at first I resisted, but in the end the evidence overwhelmed me; and now I find myself drowning in an ocean of evidence, I find myself flailing about in the eddies and currents of damaged lives. There are exceptions, of course, there is hope, there are some wonderful, skilled parents, but they are not in the majority. And why do the rest have kids? That's what I want to know. They appear to hate them. They mutilate them. They even kill them. Why do they bring these kids into the world? And why do they want to destroy them? Their own children. Why did my mother—of all people, a woman with no aptitude for the delicate, complex and exhausting task of shaping a human life, a spoiled, self-indulgent, selfish, erratic woman, a woman who should have been an artist of some kind, regurgitating her insides onto paper or canvas, a woman who should have entered a convent and shut out forever the world that was driving her mad—have children? The truth is she lacked alternatives. She was the wrong sex in the wrong place at the wrong time. *She was a woman in London Ontario in the middle of the twentieth century.* She was genetically geographically and chronologically doomed. A man as crazy as this difficult brilliant woman would have found a wife to support him and protect him and enable him to go into the world, a wife who would sacrifice her life for him—such conjunctions occur all the time. The truth is that my mother needed a wife! A sacrifice, a sacrificial lamb. She found my father, a respected physician, and she married him and gave birth to me and my brother. My father was no lamb. He was tough and aggressive and dominated those around him. He was not unlike my brilliant cousin in this regard. And yet for reasons of his own he made the sacrifice when asked. And my mother was not shy about asking. And asking and asking. The pressure was constant and incredible. She was at him night and day. She was relentless. She was devastating. In a few years, my hard-working physician father was up to three packs a day and almost three hundred

pounds. And he didn't mind. He was a doctor, after all. The truth
is he loved it! He was addicted to guilt responsibility and
exhaustion. That's why he chose my mother. She was his worthy
adversary. She was his fix. But in the end he overreached
himself. He underestimated the burden and overestimated his
own resources. In the end, he was crushed by the weight of this
chosen responsibility. He did not protest, nor did he reproach
her, he simply dropped dead. In this he was a modern man. In this
he was, at least for me, a tragic hero. He took care of her, he took
care of his patients, he took care of the boys, he took care of
everyone but himself. She took care of that. It was her first
killing. I was next on the list. *But I made a run for it.* So she went
on to my poor brother. And he is now dead. I should point out,
in all fairness, that although she beat me up a few times, in truth,
I was not molested or physically abused. The assaults were more
sophisticated, more subtle, more insidious. Even while my father
was still alive, for example, she literally managed to misplace me
on several occasions. I remember one time when I was five
finding myself alone and lost in downtown London Ontario. A
man I never saw before stopped his car and told me to get in. I
got in. He drove me home. He had heard about me on the radio.
I was reported missing. They were dragging the Thames River for
my body, he told me. Why? I asked. Someone had seen me down
by the river he said. Nowadays, I would be one of the kids who
gets snatched away and sold on the illegal adoption market, one

of the country's expanding business enterprises, but in those days, strangers picked you up and took you home and did not take you to the secret kid auctions in Toronto and Montreal. My mother had apparently taken me shopping and left me somewhere. I was misplaced many times. Even back then she was trying to get rid of me. Not consciously. It just seemed that she didn't have the concentration to keep track of her little boy—this university educated woman with a certain facility in languages and a physical resemblance to the Queen of England just happened to have a short attention span when it came to her son. And now, ironically, I have lost track of her, she is the one who is lost in London Ontario. And nobody is broadcasting her description on the radio. I remember the night I made my run. I was twelve years old. Without warning she burst into my room and said that it was now *all going to come down on us*. What? I asked. All of it! she screeched. You'll see, you'll see, she screeched. She dragged me into the kitchen where she methodically smashed every dish cup and glass in our possession. This performance, which went on for an eternity, filled me with terror. When she had finished her final dish she turned and gave me a murderous look. I took off for the bathroom and locked myself in. She followed and shouted for me to open up. She began to pound at the door with a hammer. I remember the head of the hammer splintering through the wood panels of the door. I knew if she got through that door she was going to kill me. My brother was hiding somewhere. He was good at hiding. Too good. Without thinking about it, I unlocked the door, ripped it open, sprinted past her and ran out of the house. I ran into the night, I ran through the twisting streets of London Ontario, I ran for my life. A voice inside me said: *You must not do this, you must not run, something horrible will happen if you run, something even more horrible than death.* And I was afraid of this voice. And I almost stopped. But then I thought about my mother and the dishes exploding on the kitchen floor and I kept running. And nothing horrible happened. The voice was lying. The voice, I know now, was the voice of London Ontario. I learned a lesson that night: *you can always make a run for it.* I am forever amazed when people in despair don't make a run for it. You just rip open the door and run for it. I remember back around the time of my particular run there was an abundance of adult suicides in London Ontario. These were the years before teen suicides, but it seemed like a kind of fad nevertheless. I personally knew several families afflicted by suicide, and I heard of many more. Not a month went by without a high-rise leap, a monoxide job in the garage, a bullet in the brain, an overdose of sleeping pills or a hanging. The suicide was usually a successful individual, apparently content, who gave no indication that he or she found life too unbearable to live. People in London Ontario seemed perplexed by these suicides. They hadn't noticed that life in London Ontario was loathsome, that they were living terrible lies in order to survive from day to day in London Ontario. And I don't blame them. Who wants to notice something like that? Many who did notice killed themselves or, like my mother, swelled the rosters of the mentally ill. There were also some, it goes almost without saying, who saw London Ontario for what it was and loved it. They enjoyed living terrible lies, and still enjoy it. They are the people, like certain members of my family, who thrive in London Ontario. What still puzzles me after all these years is the rueful inability of the miserable ones, the ones who noticed where they were and hated it, to make their run. It was as if the world outside London Ontario did not exist as a possible refuge. They knew the outside world was there, but they did not believe it was real. The voice of London Ontario said to them: *There is nothing out there, if you leave me something horrible will happen.* And they believed the voice. Take my Uncle Theodore, one of the hangings. Uncle Theodore worked in the family manufacturing business. They were in packaging: vacuum, stretch, shrink, clam shells, blisters, poly-bag, form-fill—containment of every kind. Uncle Theodore did it in the office during lunch hour. He used the belt off his pants. Nobody could understand it. Theodore was a nice guy, well-liked and unusually quiet. He was famous for his silences. Theodore was my grandmother's son, my mother's brother. His death broke my grandmother's heart. They did not tell her it was a suicide. They lied to her. They told her it was an industrial accident. But she knew. She knew everything. When he was alive Theodore was respected as a fair and wise man. One day he took me aside and asked me about my plans. I told him I wanted to go to university and study literature. He told me to go to the technical college and get into TV repair. That's where the future is, he told me. He said this to a kid who had trouble replacing flashlight batteries. He meant well. But he was inviting me to get lost in the contorted streets of London Ontario. They all mean well when they are inviting you to get lost. When I learned of Uncle Theodore's death, I thought about his vocational advice. I still do. Uncle Theodore was survived by his son who also committed suicide. This son got totally lost in London Ontario. After he flunked out of school, he couldn't or wouldn't find a job. He began to do community work. He joined something called the Volunteer Traffic Patrol. He would drive around town looking for people that needed assistance with their vehicles and then he would help them change a tire, or radio for help or simply give them directions—he knew intuitively that people were getting lost in London Ontario. One night while cruising through the twisting streets looking for someone to help, he ran over a young girl and killed her. It was not his fault said the courts, but he never recovered from the shock of taking a human life. A few years later he too was dead. Uncle Theodore also left a daughter behind. She now works in one of London Ontario's burgeoning psychiatric hospitals. As for Uncle Theodore's wife, a good-looking woman with a voice like a siren, I remember her vividly. She used to stroll around at family gatherings poking and squeezing tits. I remember her poking the tits of my aunts and female cousins, she even poked my mother's tits. She was greatly concerned about the way that all these tits looked. She preferred a pointy look for tits and would recommend certain brassieres that gave tits a pointy look. She talked endlessly about each set of tits and the way they should look. She was listened to with horror and respect. She told my mother that she should go for a more pointy look. Appearances are important to the people of London Ontario, I reflected, holding the letter that ruined my day. This woman, the wife of Uncle Theodore, often threw parties for her daughter, the same daughter who now works in a psychiatric hospital, which coincidentally is one of the psychiatric hospitals frequented by my mother. The wife of Uncle Theodore wanted her daughter to be popular and attractive, to be brilliant and sexy, to be devastating. She thrust her daughter into the social scene, her good-hearted but ordinary daughter, a girl preoccupied with party dresses, make-up and hair, a girl with a mind untouched by books, music, thought and the entire history of humankind. For a while it all seemed to work: she got dated and was often seen at significant teen occasions. She was popular, very very very popular, her mother repeated at family gatherings as she squeezed and prodded the available tits. But then her daughter double-crossed her: the girl began to vomit. In short order she vomited herself down to an astonishing state of emaciation. I would estimate that she plunged through the eighty-pound zone by her eighteenth birthday. Nobody could understand it. Her mother took her to a respected physician who prescribed mood-altering medications; her father, not yet a suicide, bought her a car. At night, stoned on antidepressants and munching laxative candies, she would cruise the drive-ins for jumbo shakes burgers and fries. Then she would drive to Springbank Park, get out of the car disappear behind a tree and puke. Sometimes I was invited along for the ride. After all, I was family. I was amazed and terrified by the prodigious volume of organic matter moving in and flowing out. I expected her to starve to death. But finally she rebounded and stabilized at ninety pounds—a skeleton in a flesh-coloured shrink-wrap. I lost touch with her after her father's suicide. She disappeared into the peristaltic streets. She should have made a run for it. But it never occurred to her. Decades later I bumped into her at the psychiatric hospital, her place of employment. She was charming now, pleasant, a pleasure to talk with. She had been married and divorced once or twice. She was not thin. She had learned to stomach London Ontario. Not much else to report. I asked her about her mother, the old tit-squeezer. Her mother had moved to Alaska and opened a boutique featuring foundation garments. Her mother had made a run for it. Life's full of surprises. Uncle Theodore could have made a run for it, too. He had money, he had a car, he knew how to drive. But he didn't know the way out.

PROPERTY

71

He was lost in London Ontario. And he wanted to leave. So he put a belt around his neck and took the emergency exit out of London Ontario, he stepped off his desk into the thin air of London Ontario. Uncle Theodore's wife, on the other hand, made a successful run. This simple and comic woman saw London Ontario for what it was and left. And why not? Running for it is a simple act, as simple as telling the truth. There are those who would call running for it an act of cowardice, I suppose, but I call it an act of courage, an act of survival. And as I sat in Vancouver holding the letter from London Ontario in my hands, I reflected that I was lucky to be alive. I read on: *I am writing to ask you to take care of the grounds*. I had suspected from the first, when I read the name and return address on the envelope as it lay on the wood floor, that the amicable Robert Crow was not writing out of any personal affection for me. And my suspicions were now confirmed. Bob wanted me to cut the lawn! I am living in Vancouver 2,077 miles away and Bob wants me to cut the lawn in London Ontario. My mother, wherever she is, is several thousand miles closer to the lawn than I, but Bob wants me to give it a trim. My mother is the legal tenant, and the law states, more or less, that the legal tenant is responsible for the lawn. My mother, of course, characteristically observes the law in much the same way as I observe the Fifth Commandment. In any case, misguided Bob doesn't know she's the legal tenant, he thinks it's *her* property, the first sentence of his letter established that definitively, but still he feels that I should hustle down to the airport, buy a ticket, fasten my seat belt, hail a cab, motor on over to the looping swerves of Blackpool Drive and shove the lawnmower up and down a few times. In Bob's cosmology you cut your mother's lawn—for life. In Bob's cosmology you cut your mother's lawn no matter what. That is the law of the lawn, that is the law of London Ontario. Lawndon Ontario. Lawn Done Ontario. All good citizens obey the lawn. Only outlaws and perverts, like Mom and me, disobey the lawn. Bob is merely trying to enforce the lawn. Bob thinks I should pack my lawnmower take the midnight special grab a limo and clip the lawn in the morning. Do you know how much that would cost, Bob? Are you crazy, Bob? And the worst thing about it is that I have a raging desire to do just that. I am seized by an urge to grab a cab, go to the airport, fly to London Ontario, grab a cab and cut the lawn. Swoop into London Ontario and solve something, anything, nail it down, fix it, kill it off, get it right for Mom. Simple as that. I laughed out loud at this. I said to myself: *You devised your simple plan to sell the property and give your mother an income for the rest of her life. You thought that would work. And now you dare to imagine that you could make your way into London Ontario and cut the lawn. You thought it was going to be different last summer. You told them your plan to sell the property and set up a nice income for your mother and they said bully for you. And you went to the psychiatric hospital and talked to your mother and got the power of attorney for yourself and your brilliant cousin. That was pretty well it, right. You just had to clean up the house a bit and make it saleable. What could be easier?* And so I went and cleaned up the house. Ariadne and I cleaned up the house. And we paid to have the truckloads of garbage and shit, not to mention much of the documentary history of the family, taken to the dump. And at night we stayed out in the distant suburbs with my brilliant cousin and his wife, who coincidentally works in a psychiatric hospital, although not one of those belonging to my mother. Now that I think of it almost everyone in London Ontario is in some way associated with psychiatric hospitals. Madness is a major undertaking in London Ontario. Consider the unemployment that would result if people weren't going nuts in London Ontario. Madness makes the wheels turn in London Ontario. By the end of my stay last summer I was mad, too. The real truth is that I was mad from the beginning. Only a madman without any regard for his own history could have imagined that a simple dream, or any dream, would come true in this particular family. Only a madman would have ever returned to London Ontario! Once you make a run for it, and get out alive, you should stay out. But I was so busy cleaning out the Augean stables that I didn't notice I was mad. The double-cross was right there in front of my face, but I was too deranged to see it. Like many madmen I chose instead to see what was not there. I chose the dream. And although I blame my brilliant cousin who engineered the charming little betrayal which led to the ultimate failure of my dream, and although I blame myself for having hope for telling the truth for naïvety stupidity and blindness, and although I blame London Ontario for almost everything, I place the real blame for the disaster on the CBC, the Canadian Broadcasting Corporation. It was the CBC that sucked me into the mess in London Ontario, I reflected, as I sat at my kitchen table holding the partially read letter that had ruined my day. Canada is a country that provides for certain geographical strategies. When I moved to Vancouver some time ago, I did so in order to put some distance between myself and London Ontario. The dark mountains provided a certain psychic protection that I found comforting. When one lives in Vancouver, there is only so much one can do to alleviate a problem that might arise in London Ontario, a lawn or something; one has, so to speak, an arm's length relationship with London Ontario. But when the CBC chose me as a participant in the Collaborative Vision, and began flying me to Toronto every other week or so, I found myself drawn once again into the entanglements of London Ontario, just down the highway from Toronto, just a rentacar away. I was swooping into Toronto every other week or so to save the world of television and I figured I might as well save my mother, too. There is something about people who swoop down from the heavens. Sometimes they try to save everybody, sometimes they drop bombs. The results are frequently similar. I don't think all this flying around and swooping down that everyone is doing nowadays is very good for people. The human body wasn't made to fly through the air at high speeds. I think it's driving them all mad. Look at the people who run this country, the business leaders, as they like to call themselves, and the politicians. Do you know what they do most of the time? They fly through the air at high speeds. They swoop down from the sky to solve somebody's problem. This drives them mad. I have no scientific proof of this, but a glance at the newspapers provides ample evidence. I am persuaded as well by personal experience. When I was younger, I lived with a flight attendant who worked for Air Canada. Quite a wonderful woman actually. But she flew through the air all the time and in retrospect I realize that she must have gone totally mad. This, no doubt, explains how she managed to live with someone like me. After we broke up, she married a well-known politician who constantly flew through the air trying to solve somebody's problem. He went mad and eventually became a provincial premier. They both flew through the air and they both went mad. They are still mad. I read about them in Toronto's national newspaper, the *Globe and Mail*. For my part, I went mad almost immediately when I started flying through the air. I swooped down to solve the problems of the CBC, and while I was at it I thought I might as well solve the problems of London Ontario. This is typical MFF (mad-from-flight) behaviour, commonly known as 'Muff' behaviour. Ariadne, who recently flew through the air to Arizona, and is currently watching the rodeo or the big cats at the Wild Kingdom in the desert, has a theory about Muffs. Your soul, she says, can't keep up with your body when you fly. If you fly across the country it takes a week for your soul to catch up. That's why you feel strange for a few days after a long flight. When you fly all the time, your soul gets left so far behind that it never catches up. It gets lost forever. And then you become a Muff. Muffs like to call themselves frequent flyers, but Muff is the correct locution. And the CBC, I reflected, is jam-packed with soulless Muffs. Only Muffs could have conceived the scheme of blowing $500,000 on a frolic such as the Collaborative Vision, I reflected, holding the letter that had ruined my day. Somehow these CBC Muffs got $500,000 to throw a party, despite the fact that the CBC is supposedly in desperate financial trouble. There were hundreds of applicants for the Collaborative Vision. The successful applicants were a special special special group, as they constantly told us. We were the chosen Muffs. The lucky Muffs. Everybody wants to write for television. Think of it, millions of people will hear your words, see your story, even on a bad night the numbers are stupendous. And of course, there is money everywhere, big money, buckets of it, just waiting to be dumped on you for writing a mere twenty-two minutes of entertainment, don't worry about the other eight minutes, they belong to the sponsor. First we will spend a few sessions mastering the high art of television writing, and then we will develop your ideas into saleable properties. You are the hope for the future of series television, said the Muffs at the CBC. You bring an exciting new energy. We welcome you. And we the Muff writers sat there at the CBC and listened to the lectures on how to write for TV. Tibor Lumex, a head Muff at the CBC, came in and gave us an overview of the industry. They introduced him as a badly needed and inspiring omnipresence. Tibor Lumex wore a beautiful grey suit but looked puffy and uncomfortable inside it. I am not a conformer, he said, I was kicked out of all the best schools. I am a child of television. I understand the medium. I grew up with the medium. I understand the responsibility of being a public broadcaster. I understand that we must reflect our cultures, our history and languages. I mean, there's nothing wrong with respecting your heritage and traditions. I'm Hungarian in origin myself, said Tibor Lumex. But it has to be popular. That's the nature of television. It has to be popular. I believe in Canada. I believe in the star system, he said. We need major stars in this country. I believe in major talent. We need to woo major talent back to this country, people like Anne Murray and Toller Cranston. When I was a student at UCLA, in the film department, I didn't take first year, he said, I took second year, and third year, and fourth year, and I got A's. And then they wouldn't give me my degree. They wouldn't give me my degree because I didn't take first year. My shows have won international awards,

I am not saying my shows have created a cultural revolution, but my shows have pushed the envelope. I am not a conformer, he said. I was in Hollywood, I was at NBC with Hector Kodak, a genius. It was a real learning experience, a chance to compete with the best in the world, to push yourself, he said. It makes you go better. It makes you go harder. The best in the world. I came back to Canada. Sure, I could have stayed in L.A. for a lot more money, he said. But Canada is my home, he said. I came back here to contribute something meaningful, he said, to make a difference. The Canadian audience likes its TV more *real* than the U.S. The Canadian audience likes more gambles. And remember there is one thing you have to understand to write for television. He paused. The writers leaned forward in their chairs. He continued. *Kids*, said Tibor Lumex, *control the set between 7:00 and 9:00*. If you understand that you understand everything. And you must care about what you do. You have to have passion, you have to have integrity, he said. There is nothing we have here at the CBC that can induce you to become whores, said Tibor Lumex. The money is not good enough. Do it because you enjoy it. Because you believe in it. Whores don't enjoy it, whores don't have passion, he said. You must have passion, I *want* you to enjoy it, he said. And remember, the secret to writing for television is to look at the schedule in the TV guide and figure out where the hole is. Then you develop your property to plug that hole. That is the here we are in. At that moment a man entered the room and whispered something in the ear of Tibor Lumex. I have to go, he said, there's a big story breaking in Ottawa, someone has hijacked a bus and driven it to the House of Parliament. And without another word, Tibor Lumex walked out of the room and was never seen again at the Collaborative Vision. Beaver Winslow, one of the chronic Muffs at the Collaborative Vision, the producer of *Scary Dinner Party*, took over with some additional tips. The purpose of a TV script is to keep the heads in front of the set, he said. If you lose head, you can kiss my ass, but you'll never work for me again, he said, or words to that effect. What do you think of TV scripts with a message? someone asked. The message of a television show is never contained in the script, said Beaver, the message is contained in the commercials. The message in a commercial is simple: if you buy, your life will be better. The goal of the TV writer is simple: he must not contradict this message. *Your job is to prepare the audience for this message.* Your life will be better—that is the message of television. If I find a message in your script, you can kiss my ass, but you will never work for me again, he said, approximately. As he spoke I got out a newspaper and looked at the Toronto theatre listings. After a day of watching television at the Collaborative Vision, I would often go to the theatre. At first I asked my fellow television writers to come along. They regarded me as if I were a pervert. Some of them, I discovered, had never been to a play in their lives. They knew TV. They learned to write for TV by watching TV. They formulated their ideas of acting by watching TV. They learned about culture, history and the human heart by watching TV. And so I would go to the theatre by myself, or with K, a Toronto theatre director, one of the few friends from my youth who was not missing alienated or dead. Afterward, over drinks, I would update K on my experiences at the CBC. The whole Collaborative Vision is devoted to repression. The message is: nothing is possible. The message is: do it the way it has always been done or fuck off. The message is: obey orders no matter how stupid or disgusting. The message is: if you are a complete hack in addition to being a whore you might get a job once in a while but don't count on it. The message is: writers are shit in this industry, scum. The message is: we don't even like writers, and in fact we prefer to give work to people who are not really writers. The message is: be nice and keep your mouth shut. The message is: mediocrities will censor and reshape your work and you better be *grateful* for that. The message is: don't think, don't notice that you are neck deep in shit, and don't ever ever ever try anything new. The message is: kiss my corporate ass. What did you expect? asked K. When they publicized this thing, I said, they made it sound different. So I applied. They said they were looking for new ideas, a change of direction, new talent, a fresh approach, a saviour. And you believed them? asked K. You believed advertisements sent out by people in the television business?

Well. Yeah, sort of, I said. This made K laugh and laugh. And who can blame him? One night, after a particularly grim session at the CBC, during which we the chosen writers watched videos in order to analyse the dramatic values of *Night Heat*, *M*A*S*H*, *21 Jump Street*, *Street Legal*, and *L.A. Law*, K took me to see a play called *Coming Through Slaughter*. The play, mounted by Necessary Angel, a theatre company for which K served as dramaturge, was performed in the Silver Dollar, a grimy bar on Spadina Avenue. Necessary Angel, like many of the best theatre companies in Canada, cannot afford to have its own theatre. The audience sat at tables or at the bar with their drinks. The work was daring, the acting was strong, the directing superb. Nothing about it indicated that if I bought something my life would be better. That in itself was a relief. Hope is a detestable commodity. And as I sat there in the audience watching, I think my soul, which must have been lingering in the sky somewhere above Pincher Creek, caught up with me. This thing should run forever, it's great, I said to K, it's a hit. We're closing, he replied. But the place is packed, I said, you're turning them away. The numbers stink, he replied. The room is too small. There's no space in the whole goddamn town to transfer. Our running costs are way beyond ticket revenue. This show is killing us. The next morning I went back to the CBC where they were spending $500,000 to teach me about the dramatic structure of *Cosby* and *Adderly* and *Danger Bay*, and as I watched the tapes of these

shows my soul got so disgusted that it left me, without the benefit
of a plane ride. I was a Muff again, a soulless Muff. The truth is
I don't even believe in the concept of a soul. The concept of a
soul is a business ploy concocted by the Churches of the world.
They tell you you've got this thing, this property, called a soul.
You've got it but it's separate from you. It belongs to you but it
doesn't really belong to you because it belongs to God. It's a
lease. The Church has the service contract on this soul. You pay
the Church for maintenance work. And I don't blame you. You
pay the Church because you think that your life, or in this case,
your afterlife, will be assured. Brilliant! They tell you you've got
property, which doesn't belong to you and probably doesn't even
exist, and they make you pay for it. Soul-care is one of the
greatest marketing strategies of all time. And although I don't
believe in the existence of the soul, I nevertheless felt it bail out
that morning as I sat watching the tapes. After lunch, we the
selected writers of Canada formed groups or quality circles, as
they are called, to discuss the development of our own properties. Each quality circle had a professional story editor. In the
world of television a story editor is a personage who *massages*
your script into shape. Say, for example, you sold the network a
property, a family drama about a young woman who goes to
medical school against the wishes of her respected physician
father who believes that there is no place for women in his
profession. One day, Dad and daughter play in the annual family

golf tournament at the club. Daughter shoots a very hot round and wins the tourney beating the pants off Dad. Dad's day is ruined. On the way home they make their customary stop and grab some take-out at the Big Burger. They are heading home in the heavy traffic on the expressway, Dad starts the old argument about women in medicine and gets himself worked up and begins to choke to death on his Big Burger. The youthful heroine pulls over and performs an emergency tracheotomy, with her nail file, right there in the car. Later in the hospital Dad whispers that maybe she does belong in the medical profession after all. And what's more, when she graduates he will take her into his own practice. I love it, I love it, says the story editor, but you don't need the golf course thing and the car thing. We'll put the whole shebang in the backyard. They are playing ping-pong at the annual family picnic. She beats the pants off him. Dad chokes on some barbecue and she cuts him open. I love it what do you think? It's not exactly what I had in mind, says the writer. Just rewrite, says the story editor, or you will never work in this industry again. The writer rewrites. The script is now ready to go. Then just before the shooting begins, the star who plays the father has a nervous breakdown. The stars of family drama often have nervous breakdowns. The star will not be available for the shoot. No problem, says the story editor. The daughter will perform the surgery on her pet cocker spaniel who chokes on a chicken bone, her absent physician father will guide her through every step of the operation by telephone or wait, I've got it, he'll send little incision diagrams to her via the family fax machine, and after the mutt is saved, the daughter will beat the pants off her mother in the ping-pong tournament! But that's not exactly what I had in mind, says the writer. We've got five days to shoot this sucker, says the story editor. Rewrite or you will never work in this industry again. That's the kind of thing a story editor does. They are paid handsomely for such work, often more than a grand per day. The CBC hired a number of these story editors to assist the writers in the development of properties. Cleigh McNabb, a gangly bearded redhead from Moose Factory, was our story editor. He led us into a room where our quality circle circled a table. He asked us to pitch our ideas one by one. It was a bit like Alcoholics Anonymous. When my turn came I pitched a comedy science-fiction series about a family of the future who have an android butler and live in a giant high-rise city. It was not a new idea, I had already written a play on the theme years earlier. But I didn't say that. I lied and said that I made up the idea on the spot. Cleigh said he hated my idea. And I didn't blame him. Later that day Cleigh came over to me and said he would help me develop my idea and we would go 50/50 on the profits. I thought you hated it I said. I told them about it, he said, and they loved it, and I realized I love it too. Everybody loves it. We'll be partners, he said. I'll tell you what to do with it, he said, how to clean it up and make it saleable. Then we'll pitch it to the network, he said. It needs some work, but I love it. This idea could really shake things up around here, he said, shaking my hand with a powerful wet grip. Sounds good, Cleigh, I said. The truth is I didn't have much interest in it. The play had been produced in Seattle long ago. It went decently but it was not a success and as far as I was concerned it was a dead property. I pitched the idea at the Collaborative Vision just for the sake of hearing my own well-trained voice. I had been confident in its inherent unsaleability. But to my mortification, my new partner Cleigh and I were resurrecting it as a saleable property. I was going to undertake work on a property that did not interest me, a property from the past that I did not care for, a property that I knew, in my heart, was bereft of life. But, I was nevertheless ready to clean it up and make it saleable. I was now a real genuine Muff, no doubt about it. And when the CBC flew me back to Vancouver, I went right to work on it. I wrote up a proposal. I called my new partner Cleigh in Toronto and read it to him. He loved it but he had a few suggestions. It needed to be more middle class, he said, in order to reflect the potential market audience. I rewrote the proposal with this in mind. I called Cleigh. He loved it, but he didn't like the stuff about pollution, too negative. I rewrote it. I called Cleigh. He thought the family should have grandparents living in the apartment and that the family should live in a suburb instead of a giant high-rise. I rewrote it. I called Cleigh. It needs a love interest, he said. I took a deep breath. Why don't you write it this time? I suggested. I'm too busy right now, he said. I thought this was 50/50, I said. Trust me, he said. The CBC flew me back to Toronto for another session of the Collaborative Vision. My new partner Cleigh and I had a warm very warm talk. I needed to rewrite, he said. No problem, I said. After the session I rented a car for another trip into London Ontario, just down the highway from Toronto, and then back to Toronto and back to Vancouver. And with each trip I was becoming a purer and purer Muff, a classic Muff. By the end of the summer, when I brought Ariadne east to help me clean up my property in London Ontario and make it saleable, I was absolutely and hopelessly mad. I thought I was going to sell my property. I thought I was going to make my property saleable and sell it, I thought I was going to set up a nice little income for Mom, I thought I was going to sell a series to the CBC, I thought it was all finally going to come together, I reflected, one year later, holding the letter from Bobby Crow in my hands, the letter about the thriving lawn of my unsold property on a errant street in London Ontario. *When your mother was in the house,* Bob continued, *a neighbour and I often cut the grass and my wife trimmed the bushes and helped her in the garden. Because this gave her pleasure to sit in her yard and enjoy the garden, we didn't mind doing it. But now that she is no longer resident in the house we do not feel it is our responsibility.* A disturbing passage, a mendacious passage, a bullshit passage, I reflected. And now, finally, a vestige of my one and only meeting with big Bob began to emerge from the Cimmerian depths of my mangled memory. Sure you cared about my mother's pleasure, Bob, sure you thought it was your responsibility. I hear you Bob. You thought my mother's pleasure was your responsibility! And so you and your wife and the anonymous neighbour did all these good deeds. Expecting nothing in return. You guys are practically martyrs! You invested your precious time and energy, all for my mother's pleasure, so she could sit in the garden and enjoy it. I sure hope you don't feel in your heart that your good deeds were wasted. I sure hope you don't feel ripped off. The truth is that you and your wife and the anonymous neighbour got off easy. Others have been worn out serving, others have gone mad, others have died serving, I thought, as I sat at my kitchen table, holding the letter. And as I considered Bob's words, I finally remembered the unsettling thing about my chat with Bob. The mind works in mysterious ways. I finally remembered that bleary Bob, this obscurely blond and apparently congenial man, with his balmy boyish charm, had said almost exactly the same thing when I had met him briefly last summer during my mad and frenzied journey through the maze that is called London Ontario. He had uttered the same words: pleasure, helped, bushes, enjoy, trimmed, yard, responsibility. And then, and this was the thing that was not in the letter, Bob had gone on to say he would be *very interested in buying the property!* It was a creepy moment; one that I comprehended on the spot. For Bob had obviously heard somewhere that little old ladies like my mom prefer to sell their property to a nice helpful neighbour rather than bother with those troublesome real-estate folks. Bob had heard somewhere that little old ladies like my mom often sell their houses at a price well below market value because they are grateful in their dotage for freebie gardening jobs and the like, that they feel obligated to do those nice young people a favour. The truth is amicable Bob and his incognito wife, having devoted themselves to all that compassionate trimming and cutting, felt they deserved to pick up my mother's property on the cheap. Vague Bob and his evasive better half thought my mother might be willing to forfeit fifty or sixty thousand in return for a little help in the backyard. Kindly Bob even thought he might enlist my assistance to make this happen. Poor Bob, I'm sure my mother led you on in some way. You didn't know you were dealing with a pro. You didn't know that it was not even her property! It's *my* property Bobby baby. Mom is the legal tenant. Bob, you would have had a better chance scoring with a lottery ticket. And as I sat there at my kitchen table, I also abruptly recalled the other helpful neighbour, referred to in Bob's letter, a bony little weasel, about fifty years old, who lived with his father, probably incestuously, in the house up the street. I do not remember his name. He came over one day and also told me about all the things that he had done for Mom—cutting and trimming and whatnot. And then in the next breath he offered me ninety thousand for the house on the spot. About seventy thousand below market value. He said he would fix it up, make it nice. He seemed to think this a sufficient reason, along with all the work he had done for my mother, for me to essentially throw away the property. My brilliant cousin, as I discovered eventually, had his reasons as well for wanting me to throw away the property. That's how it is with property: people act irrationally, people act selfishly, people act stupidly. And I include myself. My little chats with Bob and the weasel were appalling. I repressed them promptly. Now, however, the stimulating presence of Bob's day-ruining letter brought them back to me. Mom's little helpers are no longer helping. And, I reflected, the plant life on the property is inexorably expanding and petrifying the neighbours the street and let's face it the entire municipality of London Ontario. The truth is I would have been delighted to sell the property to any devoted cutter-of-lawns and trimmer-of-bushes who made a decent offer. But I cannot sell. I own the property but I cannot sell it! The law is clear. The codicil appended with a pin on the baby-blue cardboard binder of the will gave my mother a life interest in the property. The law states: *A grantor in a deed or will may grant an interest in the lands to someone for a time period. That interest will cease at the death of the named individual, e.g. 'to A for his life' or 'to A until B dies.'* Perfectly clear. Them lawyers sure can write. In other words Mom has the final say. At the time, last summer, I did not think this was a problem. I had the power of attorney, that is to say, I had the power of attorney *along with* my brilliant cousin, and my mother said she wanted me to sell the house. She told me so when I visited the psychiatric hospital. And so I went to London Ontario, with Ariadne in hand, with my power of attorney in hand, and began cleaning out the shit and garbage. I was making the house saleable. I was ready to sell. I was ready to set Mom up for life. And one day I called a real-estate company and in less than ten minutes Don the real-estate guy pulled into the driveway. There's no business like property business, I reflected, holding the letter that had entered my hall and ruined my day. If you needed a heart transplant or something, it could take months to get a doctor's appointment, never mind the operation; similarly, you could die of old age before you get a date with, say, an electrician, a plumber, or a carpenter; but with property you get *action*, I reflected, as I stood up, walked over to the garbage receptacle under the sink and hurled Bob's letter into a mixture of wet coffee grounds, rotting banana peels and coagulating porridge. I did not plan this. It just happened. And I immediately regretted it for I was curious about the remainder of his letter. I hesitated, and then with revulsion I withdrew the now sticky and moist object from my garbage receptacle. A brown clump of ground coffee, bearing a resemblance to human faeces, adhered to the face of the page. I brushed it off with my hand leaving brown and yellow streaks on the paper. I washed my hands. I conveyed the letter that had ruined my day to the front hall and then out through the front door, the same front door which had admitted it in the first place, and onto the front porch where I sat in a sturdy Adirondack chair. I placed the letter from Robert Crow, the letter that had once entered but had now left my house, on the wide wooden arm of the sturdy Adirondack chair so that it might dry. I leaned back on the wooden slats of my sturdy Adirondack chair and studied a white baby-mattress sky. *Baa, baa, black sheep*, I sang, *have you any wool? Yes sir, yes sir, three bags full*. The consuetudinary ritual of the telephone interrupted from within. I counted. The caller hung on for seventeen rings. Clearly not a person I wished to talk with. I will not talk with anyone who rings seventeen times. I then thought about returning to the interior of the house and disconnecting, but I found that I was now completely possessed by the sturdy Adirondack chair, with its sloping back and deep slanted seat, and I could only lean back and wait. My mother, the one time she visited Vancouver, had complained that there was not a comfortable place to sit in my entire house. She did not approve of the chairs in my house. Now, as I sat on my porch, giving my body completely to my Adirondack chair, I recalled her complaints. She had come in 1986. She had come for the purpose of seeing Expo '86. Her visit unfortunately occurred before Ariadne purchased the Adirondack chair in 1989. I think my mother would not have complained so much if the Adirondack chair had been there for her. She always liked a nice outdoor chair. There were nice outdoor chairs for her in the backyard in London Ontario. And she would often sit out there for many hours. In the warm weather she spent most of her time in the yard, partly, as affable Bob suggested, because she enjoyed it, but fundamentally because she could not stomach the filthy chaos that she had created in the house. And I don't blame her. The truth is she would go to the psychiatric hospital every winter, and more recently in the summer as well, because she could not bear to actually occupy the interior of the house she legally occupied in London Ontario. My house. She preferred to go to the psychiatric hospital, usually in an ambulance, rather than clean the house. Nor would she allow anyone else to come and clean the house. I tried many times to hire house cleaners, but she would always drive them away. She was embarrassed by the condition of the house. She could not bear the thought of a stranger seeing such a mess. And I don't blame her. It was okay with Mom if I saw the mess, of course, because I was family. It doesn't matter what family thinks. But the rest of the world counts. The world, that is, of London Ontario. And in fact, in the past, whenever I visited her during holidays, I would spend my entire vacation cleaning, disinfecting, scrubbing, throwing out the papers and garbage, scraping out the filth and shit. Each time it would cost me more than one thousand dollars to travel to London Ontario and clean. I was the thousand-dollar cleaning lady. Last summer's excursion was traditional in this respect. On the other hand, as Ariadne and I cleaned the house in order to make it saleable, I sincerely believed that this was the last time that I would ever go through the papers filth and shit of my mother's life. I thought that I was taking an action, and that it would have the intended result. This alone proves that I was mad. For no action involving my mother ever has its intended result. How could I think that I was about to change this pattern? The hubris of it! It is as if I presumed to alter a veritable law of nature—Mom's First Law: *for every action there occurs an absurd and regrettable reaction.* My mother's visit to Vancouver plainly demonstrates the veracity of this law. She said she wanted to see Expo '86. I invited her to Vancouver for the purpose of seeing Expo '86. But she did not see Expo '86. She got to Expo '86, but she did not see Expo '86. She almost saw it, but at the last moment she did not. She went there, to the Expo site, but she saw nothing. When she phoned me from London Ontario and said she wanted to see Expo '86, I believed her. I believed the woman who practically invented the art of lying. I was suspicious, but, I reassured myself, why would she lie about a thing like that? I picked her up at the airport. She was going to be with us for ten days. I took her to my Vancouver house, the one owned by the bank. I brought friends over to meet her. They liked her. My mother can be a charming woman. As for Ariadne and me, my mother essentially ignored our existence. When

Ariadne attempted a conversation, my mother would give her a curt word or two and then head for the bathroom. When I tried to talk with her she stared straight ahead and pressed her lips together until they turned white. My mother prefers strangers, she prefers those whom she does not know, or, to be precise, she prefers those who do not know her. And I don't blame her. During her stay with us, she slept between sixteen and eighteen hours each day. But she was not entirely silent, for several times she found it necessary to complain about the lack of comfortable chairs in my house. Each morning, I would offer to take her to Expo '86. But she would only shake her head and mutter about tomorrow. After six days of sleeping, of charming my friends, of complaining about the lack of comfortable seating, of snubbing Ariadne and me, my mother announced that she was at last ready to see Expo '86. And so on the seventh day of her trip to Vancouver I paid the twenty-dollar-per-person-admission and entered the west gate of Expo '86. I was disgusted to be there. This so-called world exposition, that was nothing more than a hyped-up trade show, represented everything that I detest about our civilization. It was all machine-worship, and blinking lights, and metal tubes, and lineups, and bad food, and tasteless pavilions, and sleazy fast-buck operators, and Christian businessmen, and amateur street theatre, and lurid souvenirs, and wasted money. The whole city had gone mad. Everybody thought they were going to get rich by latching onto the action. The message of

Expo '86 was simple: *We are whores in B.C., come and fuck us in the bum*. And that, in the end, is just what happened, but on a scale that surprised even me, for in the end, Expo '86 turned out to be one of the great property scams of all time. The government sold the site, which comprised a good chunk of downtown Vancouver, to a respected Hong Kong businessman, for a paltry sum. The government threw away a good chunk of downtown Vancouver, some of the most valuable real estate in the world, for a quick cash fix. It has been said that the Indians who sold Manhattan got a better deal than the Province of British Columbia got on the Expo '86 site. And when the government sold the property, the buyer from Hong Kong demanded that the government agree to clean up the property, because there was some question of industrial pollution on the site. And the government agreed, they agreed to clean up the property and make it saleable. And who can blame them? And now in the end it appears that the clean-up alone will cost the government more than they made on the land deal. Ah well. That's property for you. But as I walked onto the grounds of what was to become one of the great property scams of all time, accompanied by my mother, and Ariadne, and filled with loathing and revulsion, I nevertheless resolved that I would overcome my disgust and attempt to show my mother a good time; I resolved that I would feign enthusiasm for the pathetic exhibits, that I would keep my doubts and reservations about the stupid and hateful pretense of

Expo '86 to myself. And as I stood there in the west entrance before a silver dome which reminded me of the eye of an insect, I said to myself: I will be a good boy, I will give her pleasant memories to take back to London Ontario. She has not had a happy life, this woman, but today she will have a brief interlude of happiness. I am an actor, a trained actor, I said to myself, a trained liar, a professional liar, and I am capable of making this a day to remember. I will take an action, and it will have the intended result. As I made these resolutions I noticed that my mother was no longer standing beside me. I looked down and discovered that she was lying flat on her back on the concrete. Her face was white and she was still. *My God*, I thought, *my mother has died at Expo '86*. I knelt down and held my mother in my arms. Mother, I said, Mother. She was stiff in my arms. I was trembling. Ariadne knelt beside us. What is it? What's wrong? she said. I don't know, I said, I don't get it. I could not believe this was happening. Don't move her, a voice said in a strong American accent. I looked up at a black woman of indeterminate age. I'm a nurse, she said, I'll get help. She disappeared. *I have killed my mother at Expo '86*, I thought, *I forced my mother to come to Expo '86 and she died. She wanted to stay home and sleep but I forced her to come to Expo '86 and die*. Suddenly her body interrupted my thoughts, emitting a long shivering moan. She was still alive! By this time a crowd had gathered to watch. My mother and I had become a new exhibit at Expo '86. A clown, one of Expo's paid street-entertainers, came over and began to mock her as she lay unconscious and moaning in my arms. I told him to piss off. I screamed at him. I called him an asshole. He left reluctantly making cute little clown faces. I am always amazed at the arrogance and insensitivity of my colleagues in the theatre. If I had a gun I probably would have shot him. The training of theatre performers in this country is a scandal. By now the paramedics were on the scene and they loaded my mother into a little electric car and we all went down a ramp to an exceedingly well-equipped and well-staffed infirmary hidden deep within the bowels of Expo '86. These people, all dressed in white, were delighted to see my unconscious mother. They were bored, they were tired of sitting around in their stunningly well-equipped infirmary secreted under Expo. I live in a province with an endemic shortage of trained hospital staff and hospital beds, and meanwhile at Expo '86, the money toilet of the century, a dozen qualified medical staff, nurses, paramedics, orderlies and at least one doctor, are sitting on their asses day after day, waiting for someone like my mother to pay a visit. They all grouped around her bed and tested and prodded her and rubbed her wrists and attached her to machines. My mother regained consciousness and looked around calmly. She seemed right at home. *Are you taking any medications?* a nurse asked her. I don't know, my mother replied in a tiny little girl voice. *Did you have any medications?* I'm not sure, my mother replied. *Did you have any medications today?* Well, maybe I did. *What medications?* Just a little nitroglycerin for my heart. Dr. Frisch gave it to me. He's one of the finest doctors in London Ontario. He's been looking after me for some time. He's actually from Vienna. He's one of many respected doctors in London Ontario. My husband was a doctor too. *How much did you take?* Oh, maybe a little extra, just to get me through the day. *I think we better get you over to Saint Paul's.* And so the ambulance came and took my mother to Emergency at Saint Paul's. By the time I got there, a half-hour later, my mother actually knew the names of the doctors in the emergency room, not to mention a few nurses. They were all her new pals. And she was happy lying there enthroned in bed with a little white curtain around her. She was in a hospital and she was happy. My mother had O.D.'d on nitro, in order to help her through the day at Expo '86, and now she was in the hospital, and she was happy. I thought she had died, but she hadn't. Nevertheless she went straight to heaven. Hospital heaven. My mother introduced me to her new pal Dr. Sullivan. She'll be fine, said the good doctor, the nitro just lowered her blood pressure a bit, that's all. And he was right. A few hours later they discharged my mother and we drove back to the house and she went to bed. That was her trip to Expo '86. Mom's First Law held up just fine on that one. When she eventually got back to London Ontario she told her friends and family that she had a very good time at Expo '86 and even described some of the exhibits. She did not bother to mention she had not seen Expo '86. She did not bother to mention that she had incurred a substantial medical bill. In any case, the bill was paid by the medicare system, which has supported my mother's institutional habits over the last forty years. I once calculated, while sitting in my front hall staring at the front door, that my mother had cost the medical system more than a million dollars during her medical career. It would have been far cheaper for them to just give her a decent therapist and a proper course of treatment in the first place. In fact I once asked Dr. Frisch why he kept fooling around with brain-destroying shock therapy, mind-numbing antidepressants and endless futile groups when a traditional one-on-one with a good shrink might have actually done something to help her. He said, and I quote, the health care system is under too much stress for that kind of thing. Besides, he added, your mother is not a likeable person. And so instead the system had to cough up over one million dollars. The people of Canada thank you, Dr. Frisch. They thank you for blowing a million dollars of their money. With a million dollars Dr. Frisch, you could have installed her in a luxury apartment with a series of housekeepers for Her Highness to abuse and all would have been well. She would have lived happily ever after. There would have been money left over, I reflected. You could have given yourself a raise, Dr. Frisch. With that kind of money my mother could have even bought me a comfortable chair or two and improved her

Vancouver holiday immeasurably. But she did not have that luxury, and now with her tour of Expo '86 complete, she became even more vituperative about the difficulties of finding a proper place to sit. There is no place to sit in your house, said my mother, it's horrible. A house without comfortable seating is not a house, said my mother, it's just a place to stay out of the rain. I don't know how you live like this, said my mother—the same mother who did such a dynamite bang-up job keeping up her own house, which is actually my house, in London Ontario, the same mother who scorched the floors, opened fissures in the walls, clogged the plumbing with rotting food, accumulated mountains of cat shit, garbage, old newspaper and so much more. I don't know how you live like this, she said. On the morning of her scheduled departure for London Ontario, I peeped into her room and discovered that she had not yet packed. I took in the scene: clusters of stockings hideous and epidermal, tortured undergarments, wadded-up newspapers, divers psychotropic medications, a brown banana half eaten, assorted plastic bags containing every imaginable and unimaginable personal effect. Two large suitcases lay empty and abandoned amidst the rubble. My mother was standing at the dressing table pushing, from one place to another, small articles of recently acquired booty, mostly air travel plethora: toothpicks, napkins, plastic cutlery, minute packages of salt and pepper, peanuts, little rosettes of used Kleenex, a vomit bag and a brochure that explained where the emergency exits were located. Mom looked like she was right at home. I went back into my room sat on the bed and stared at the floor. Her plane was leaving in less than two hours. She was not ready. She would miss her plane. She would never leave. I would soon be dead. Ariadne appeared. You look catatonic, she said. She isn't packed, I replied, her stuff is all over the place. What are you going to do? asked Ariadne. I did not answer. Ariadne went in to have a talk with my mother. My mother explained that it was time for a bath and went into the bathroom and slammed the door. I continued to stare at the floor. Ariadne, however, took advantage of the opportunity. She threw my mother's possessions, clothes, newspapers, litter, into the suitcases. When my mother finally emerged from the bath, Ariadne somehow managed to get her dressed. We were now less than one hour from departure. It takes thirty minutes to drive to the airport. I continued to stare at the floor. Then, miraculously, Ariadne had my mother moving down the stairs. My mother was coughing now. She was developing a serious cough. I grabbed the suitcases, ran out to the car, started the engine. Slowly Ariadne and my mother emerged from the house. Ariadne got my mother into the car. Forty minutes remained. I drove to the airport. Somehow I did not have a car accident. And I have been known to have car accidents when traversing the physical and/ or metaphysical zone of my mother's influence. One time, after a dispute with my mother, I hit a lamppost not one hundred yards from the house on a bend in Blackpool Drive. The paint from my car still scars that lamppost, evidence of a susceptible and demented psyche. Another time, after a lively interchange with my mother, I had a head-on collision with what turned out to be a very important and respected physician in London Ontario. I was lucky to survive. Last summer, after visiting my mother at the psychiatric hospital, I almost ran over a woman at a crosswalk. The truth is I almost *backed* over her. I had stopped mid-inter-section after realizing that I was running a red light. I put it in reverse and stepped on the gas. Fortunately K, my theatre friend from Toronto, who happened to be with me that day, saved the woman's life by screaming at me to stop. Others have succumbed to my mother's charms. No one is immune. After the nitro-induced collapse to the concrete at Expo, for example, Ariadne, while driving to the hospital, literally knocked the groceries out of a woman's hands with the car. She broke the woman's eggs. Ariadne stopped the car, gave the woman twenty dollars and drove on. Such things happen when traversing the perilous zone. Nevertheless, on the morning of my mother's return flight to London Ontario, I managed to pull up safely in front of the terminal. My mother then refused to get out of the car. She said she needed a wheelchair. During the ride to the airport she had apparently lost the use of her legs. Ariadne went off to find a wheelchair. The plane was leaving in ten minutes. After threatening several airport officials with bodily harm, Ariadne returned with a wheelchair. The helpful airport police leaned in and told me to move on or they would tow my car. I began to laugh hysterically. Ariadne was busily coaxing my mother into the wheelchair. I told the cops to tow to their hearts' content. I ran inside pushed my way to the front of a line and got the boarding pass. Then they wouldn't let us take her to the departure gate. Security regulations. I sprinted over to a red cap, gave him all my money, about eighty dollars, and said get that woman on her plane. A lot of money goes down the drain around my mother. The red cap rolled her through security at high speed and she was gone. She did not say goodbye. She did not say thank you. We went back for the car. It was gone. We took a cab home and went to bed. It took several days to recover from my mother's visit to Expo '86. It took us several more days to realize that my mother had not come to Vancouver to see Expo '86. She had in fact lied about that. She had no interest at all in Expo '86. The real objective of her trip was to move in with us, *permanently*. She had decided to relocate. Ariadne and I were young and strong and would serve her well. The frightening thing is that without Ariadne's iron will, it would have happened! And I would now be dead. What a lucky guy I am, I said to myself, as I sat in the sturdy and comfortable Adirondack chair on the front porch of my Vancouver house, the sturdy Adirondack chair that my mother would probably never sit in. And as I sat there thinking about my mother and Expo '86 and London Ontario and my brilliant cousin and the CBC and the disastrous clean-up of last summer and psychiatric institutions and the fact that I was still alive, I abruptly recalled Thomas Bernhard sitting in his wing-chair at his famous artistic dinner in the novel *Woodcutters*. I thought about Bernhard for several minutes, about his contempt for Vienna and its people and its theatre and its writers and its artists and its coffee-houses and its buildings and its monuments and its cobbled streets—in fact for all things Viennese. I thought about his contempt for himself. I thought about his rage. At least, I reflected, I was alone in my Adirondack chair, with the dark mountains and thousands of miles of prairie and forest protecting me from my Vienna. Whereas for Bernhard, sitting in his wing-chair among the people he hated, there was no real escape, except in his art or in sleep or in death. At least I have escaped, I said to myself, at least I have escaped I said looking at the soggy letter on the arm of the Adirondack chair, the soggy letter that ruined my day, at least I have escaped, I said again and again. Yes I have escaped. I am still alive and I have escaped, I said. I am alive. I have escaped. I said this so many times that finally I had no idea what I was talking about. And, in any case, the truth is that I had not escaped. If I had truly escaped, I reflected, I would not feel this oneiric urge to fly to London Ontario and mow the lawn of my miserable property on the meandering and maddened curves of Blackpool Drive, I would not be obsessed with the grotesque menacing turf thriving on a

property that I do not want and cannot sell, a property legally
occupied by my mother whose current whereabouts are to me
unknown. No, you have not escaped, I said to myself. You still
have your property and as long as you have your property there
is no escape. You made a run for it, I said to myself, but you have
not escaped. You have not *really* escaped. It is difficult to really
escape, I said to myself. When I finished the Collaborative
Vision at the CBC, for example, I thought that I had really
escaped. But I had not. Of course I did not go to the Collaborative Vision thinking about escape. I was a good boy at the
Collaborative Vision. I did what I was supposed to do. I developed my property and made it saleable. Finally I tried to sell my
property to the big buyers who appeared at the final session of the
Collaborative Vision. For weeks the organizers of the Collaborative Vision had talked endlessly about the coming of the
mysterious big buyers. Who are the big buyers? we the writers
asked. The big buyers, we were told, are powerful people in the
industry, decision-making people who know the business inside
out. The big buyers, we were told, are real creative types, the
best, with a whole lot of marketing savvy. And we the chosen
writers of Canada, the dynamic and indispensable and desperately needed new blood, as they kept informing us, the hope of
the future of television, that is to say of the world, as they kept
notifying us, were going to confront these sapient tycoons of
mass entertainment; we the chosen people were going to pitch

our newly developed properties; and they, the big buyers, were going to sagely critique our properties. And maybe buy them. So when the big buyers arrived finally on the final day of the Collaborative Vision there sure was a heck of a lot of excitement around. And who were the big buyers? Well, there was Franco Hermes, the co-creator of a sitcom that had run in the late sixties. Then there was Maggie Klue who worked somewhere in production at the CBC. And there was Ben Scham, a marketing exec for a rival network. And finally, there was Richie Orex, who worked as a story editor for the long-running Canadian dramatic series, *Fish Farm*, one of the most stupid and inept shows ever conceived. This élite panel sat fidgeting behind a long table. These were the big buyers. We the chosen writers sat randomly arrayed before them in all our hopeful splendour. The big buyers did not look happy. The big buyers behaved as though they had been dragged kicking and screaming to the final session of the Collaborative Vision. They looked as if they had been beaten into it. They looked aggravated and mournful about being present at the Collaborative Vision. And I didn't blame them. Then we the chosen writers began pitching our properties. The first writer pitched her property, a sitcom about a member of parliament. It doesn't have enough jeopardy, said Franco Hermes. It's too public affairs, said Maggie Klue. From a market point of view demographics are skewed, said Ben Scham. I agree with the others, said Richie Orex. So much for the first writer. The second writer pitched his property, a dramatic series about a Canadian soldier fighting in World War I. World War I is not a draw anymore, said Franco Hermes, all that gas and slogging through the mud, no one wants to see that, World War I is too low tech. Maggie Klue added: The trouble with just setting a single character in World War I is that there's not enough room for dramatic conflict. What if you changed your series so that it was about two brothers who couldn't get along? And put it in World War II. I think that World War II would work for this. Why don't you rewrite it that way? I think it would be more dramatic. Ben Scham said: Your low concept is good but your high concept is bad. What do you mean? asked the writer. Ben Scham answered: Your low concept is the thing your show is about. That has merit. But the high concept, that is to say, what other show is it *like*, is your real problem. It isn't *like* anything. If I can't say to a producer, it's like *Hogan's Heroes* or it's like M*A*S*H, how the hell do you expect me to sell it? You need a high concept to sell a new series! It needs to be *like* something. Richie Orex said: I agree with the others in everything they've said, also I think there is some kind of jeopardy problem. As these élite television professionals, the big buyers, critiqued and evaluated our properties, I listened with horror. The big buyers were idiots! They had no knowledge of dramatic structure or character or story. They had no imagination. They were positively moronic in comparison to the group of writers they were busily humiliating. These are the people who make the decisions, I thought to myself. These are the people who have made television what it is today and will continue to make it what it will be tomorrow. Then my turn came. I stood up before the big buyers and pitched my science-fiction series. I'm sorry I just don't like this kind of thing, said Franco Hermes, who once had a series in the sixties. I think there's a jeopardy problem, said Maggie Klue, who worked somewhere in production at CBC. *TV is not a pioneering medium*, said Ben Scham from the rival network. Do you think we're crazy? Science-fiction sitcom? This is TV! This is a business! *If you want to write a poem, keep it at home in the drawer!* Richie Orex of *Fish Farm* added: I have to agree with what the others have said. I sat down. Cleigh McNabb, my good pal and partner, leaned over and whispered to me that the big buyers were right, that he didn't like my property, that he had never liked my property. What an honest guy, I thought. So it was all over. And I told myself I would never do it again. I was finished with the CBC. I was humiliated. I was relieved. The next writer proposed an adventure series about a bush pilot who lives in the Canadian North and flies around and rescues people. There is some jeopardy, but not enough, said Franco Hermes. What if you rewrite it so that he flies everywhere with his gorgeous wife as co-pilot, suggested Maggie Klue. I like it, said Ben Scham. *It's real Canadian. I'm willing to option this. I think this is the right show at the right time.* The entire room burst into wild

applause. The chosen writers, the select group that was handpicked to change the direction of a sick and tired industry, went
ecstatic because a manifest imbecile said he wanted to option a
show about a bush pilot. *We are all whores here*, I thought. Well
uh, maybe I will option it, too, said Richie Orex. And then the
Collaborative Vision was over, and I believed that I had escaped
television forever. And I rejoiced. But I had not escaped. A few
weeks later there was a phone call from Conrad Shadow, the
head of something at CBC. I've just heard about your proposal
for a new science-fiction series. I love it. *So if you can just prove
to me that you can write I could get very interested.* I've already proven
that I can write, Conrad, I said. *Yeah sure, but can you write
comedy?* he said, that's the big big question to me. Conrad, I said,
have you read anything I've written? No, he said. But Conrad,
I said, I sent you guys my stuff. You got it all right there at the
CBC. *I want you to write something just for me*, replied Conrad, *I
want you to make me laugh.* Conrad, I said, fuck off. No one has
ever said that to me before, replied Conrad. Well, I said, maybe
it's about time someone did. And then I hung up. This time I've
really escaped, I thought. But next day, Conrad's assistant
phoned and said that if I got down on my knees and apologized,
those were her very words, Conrad would probably option my
show. What does that mean? I asked. It means a cheque for
several thousand dollars, she replied. I'll think about it, I said. I
still had not escaped. I wanted the money. I wanted the easy TV

money I kept hearing so much about. I wanted to sell my property and get rich. I wanted to get rich writing. What a stupid idea, I said to myself, as I sat in my Adirondack chair. How stupid to conceive of my writing as property, saleable property. Although, of course, it is property, my property, and it is something I can sell, with luck, but that is not the way to *conceive* of it. I am my writing, I reflected. My writing is me, I reflected. *And I am not property*, I said to myself. I am not for sale. And yet perhaps I was for sale at the Collaborative Vision. I put myself on the market and I was for sale. *I am property*, I said to myself. But I took myself off the market before making the sale. And I escaped. More or less. And in the end, after months of idiotic and sickening negotiations, I again told Conrad to fuck off and I again escaped. That time it worked. If you want to escape, I told myself as I sat in my Adirondack chair, you must give up all thought of selling your property. Only then will you escape. You must give up all thought of selling yourself. You must learn this and then each day you must learn it again, I said to myself, until finally it is second nature. But, I said to myself, the real truth is, if you truly want to escape, you must give up the whole idea of property. *You must give up property!* And yet, I reflected, I cannot do it. Will not. I cannot give up property. Not completely. Not yet. And so, I have not escaped. I made a run for it, I am still alive, but I have not escaped. *You can run but you can't hide*, I said to myself. *Run run run run run*, I said to myself. *Fuck property!* I said to myself. *The neighbours are getting upset*, continued the letter from Robert Crow, the letter that entered my house through the mail slot and then exited through the front door, the letter, crumpled and stained, that now lay drying on the wide arm of the Adirondack chair, the letter about my property. *The grounds are thick with bushes that need trimming*, he wrote, *and the weeds are flourishing*. Benign Bob had already used the word *grounds* once in the letter. Bob you are getting unpleasantly repetitious, I thought to myself, as I sat on my front porch in my sturdy Adirondack chair. I found his repeated use of *grounds* appalling and detestable. I often find repetition appalling and detestable. Bobby honey, we're talking here about a lawn on a run-down property on a crooked street in a modest but pretentious middle-class neighbourhood in London Ontario. It does not have *grounds*, Bob, it has a *lawn*. It is not Windsor Castle, Bob. It does not have *grounds*, and you do not have *grounds* on your property either, Bob. Some real-estate agent told you that the property had *grounds* Bob, and you chose to believe him, and you bought the place, but if you would just go out your front door and look around you would discover a front lawn Bob, you will not find *grounds*. There are no *grounds* on Blackpool Drive Bob, the real-estate agent conned you Bob, you were misled Bob, I reflected, leaning back on the wooden slats of my Adirondack chair, and as I leaned back a gust of wind lifted Bob's letter into the air and carried it off the porch. This made me laugh, although I'm not sure why. I hauled myself out of my Adirondack chair and peered over the porch railing. The letter had landed below on a juniper bush; it looked like a piece of ordinary trash. As I lumbered down the stairs to retrieve it, the wind came up again and blew it into the street. I waited patiently at the curb as several vehicles drove over it. *One for my master*, I sang, *one for my dame, but none for the little boy who cries in the lane.* I sauntered into the street and repossessed the letter that had ruined my day, stuffing it into the pocket of my greenjeans, an act that gave me pleasure, like all acts associated with my greenjeans, for I have loved and dreamed of greenjeans since I was a kid, but I could never get myself a pair, I could never get anyone to buy me greenjeans, I could not even get anyone to listen to me on this small dream. Or any other dream. I was not an acquisitive child. I rarely asked for things. But I urgently required greenjeans. They were simply crucial to me. That's how kids are. And who can blame them? I tried to save money for greenjeans out of my allowance, but I never made it. And now, at the age of forty-six, I found a pair of greenjeans and I bought them and I wear them. When I grow up I once said to myself I will buy greenjeans. No one will stop me. As time passed I of course forgot this vow. But recently, when I saw the greenjeans in the store, I remembered and I bought them. And they have given me great pleasure, just as I dreamed they would. *Sometimes things work out*, I thought as I found myself straying farther from my house. I had in fact meant to return to my

Adirondack chair to finish reading the letter now in my pocket, the pocket of my greenjeans, but instead I wandered off and lost myself in a maze of streets and alleys. *Return to your Adirondack chair!* I admonished myself. *Conclude the letter and salvage what is left of your ruined day.* But instead I found myself on Main Street where I came upon a ruckus attended by two police officers, a Chinese woman in grey business attire, and the object of their attention, an older woman, perhaps seventy, in a white sun-dress and a flat white hat. The old woman was emitting horrid screeching cries like those of an agitated parrot in a cage, pitiful cries that filled the air with torment and foreboding. I knew instantly what this sound meant for I had heard it before: it was the sound of an unwilling confrontation with a grotesque and inexorable fate. I knew what it meant, but I could not, would not, remember where I had previously heard it. And I wanted to turn away before I did remember, I wanted to escape the dominion of this terrible sound, I wanted to run from this sound and the memories it evoked. But I was paralysed. I was compelled against my will to remain and witness the agony of the woman in white. She was sparring with some invisible enemy, flailing against it with her thin white arms. Her hand brushed the jacket of one of the police officers. He looked down at the place where she had touched his uniform and examined himself, as if he had been dirtied in some way. Without warning she stepped off the curb and plunged into the vehicular traffic on Main Street. The police watched impassively. But the Chinese woman, at the risk of her own life, followed into the traffic and brought the old woman safely back to the sidewalk. The police looked annoyed. Perhaps they would have preferred to see the old woman die under the wheels of a truck. They didn't want to soil their hands, they didn't want to touch her. But the Chinese woman, who may have been a social worker of some kind, was apparently dedicated to the preservation of the woman in white. The high-pitched screeching continued and continued. And, against my will, I finally remembered where I had heard these sounds before. I had heard them in London Ontario. I remembered my mother making these very sounds as she stormed through the house tearing books and smashing lamps and throwing furniture against the wall. The woman in white started into the traffic once again but this time the Chinese woman anticipated and blocked her path. I watched the woman in white, but I could only see my mother, my frail and ageing mother, who screeched like a parrot, and tried to smash the world. *The suffering of women*, I said to myself. *The suffering of women*. I felt the words forming on my lips. *The suffering of London Ontario*. The woman in white was really in London Ontario. She was in Vancouver, but she was lost in London Ontario. She was trying to escape into the traffic. But there was no escape for her. She was trapped in London Ontario. She was my mother. *There is no escape*, I said to myself. *There is no escape*. I turned away and dragged myself back up the

lane to my property. I climbed the steps of my front porch and
momentarily considered the inviting contours of my Adirondack
chair, but instead I entered my property. I lay down on the
polished wood floor of my front hall and stared at the ceiling. I
lay with my head in the very place where the letter had fallen.
If the letter, which languished crumpled and stained in the
pocket of my greenjeans, had come through the mail slot at this
point, it would have smacked me right in the face. And as I lay
there beneath the mail slot, I began to cry and to moan and to
shake on the polished wood floor of my front hall. And I did not
know why. *I don't know why I am crying*, I said to myself, *I don't
know why*, I insisted. But in truth I knew. I was crying for the
woman in the white sun-dress, I was crying for my mother whose
whereabouts I did not know, I was crying for my physician father
who died in his forty-sixth year utterly worn out from taking care
of my mother and his two sons and his patients and the world,
I was crying for my poor brother who threw himself under the
wheels of a train after a mysterious screaming altercation with
my mother, I was crying for my brilliant cousin who might have
been a great man but instead got lost in London Ontario and
lived a secluded and unremarked life hoarding his precious
stones and his real-estate, becoming a dedicated servant of the
plutocracy in the process. I was crying for my family, a family that
had arrived in the New World at the turn of the century with
high hopes, hopes that had almost materialized, but finally had

faded and in the end were forgotten—a family that took root, grew and at length decayed, but never flowered—a family that failed. I was crying for my grandmother, the grandmother who willed me my property in London Ontario, who after more than a hundred years of life looked at her family and saw what it had become and died in disgust. I was crying for myself, an additional indulgence that filled me with self-loathing. And as I lay crying with my head on the spot where the letter had fallen, the letter that entered and exited and re-entered my house, the phone rang. I rose to my feet and toddled towards the kitchen. I counted fifteen rings and then I answered. It was Ariadne calling from Arizona. Ariadne had just returned from seeing both the rodeo *and* the big cats at the Wild Kingdom in the desert. She told me that the rodeo was revolting. The big cats, on the other hand, were magnificent. She told me she was having a wonderful time with her family. I told her about the letter that had dropped through the mail slot and ruined my day. I told her about how the lawn was proliferating in London Ontario, about how the weeds were threatening the entire region, I told her about Robert Crow's use of the word 'grounds.' Ariadne laughed. I laughed with her. We laughed in unison although we were thousands of miles apart. The telephone is an indispensable apparatus, I said to myself as I laughed, it's a great invention, I said to myself. I resolved to plug my telephone in more frequently. But then I remembered all my callers, the ones who were not Ariadne, and

I swore to unplug as soon as the call ended. This thing with my mother and that house goes on and on, I said, I cannot escape. You can escape, she replied, you've escaped before, tomorrow you will escape again. She paused. If only you had sold that property last summer, it would be easier, she said. But your stupid cousin made sure that didn't happen, she said. Your stupid cousin had to make his little point. Sure he helps your family. He likes doing it. As long as it's done his way. It makes him feel noble. But when it isn't done his way, his way exactly ... That's not why he does it, Ariadne, I said, the guy has convictions, ideas of how things should go, ideas of duty. Yeah, like when he wanted you to kill that cat. You wouldn't kill that cat. You wouldn't do your duty. He wanted you to kill that cat because he knew that if you would kill that cat for him, you would do anything. Don't worry about your scruples, just kill that cat and all will be well. And when you wouldn't, he found a way to punish you for granting that cat the boon of life. And last summer when you wouldn't go along with his program on the property, he found a way to punish you for that, too. He doesn't like cats, your stupid cousin, they do things their own way, she said. Have you ever noticed that there is no stereo in your stupid cousin's house? He doesn't like music, because music is mysterious, it's emotional, it doesn't fit into his scheme of things. But he owns a piano, Ariadne, I said. Did you ever hear him play it? she said. No, I said. Have you ever looked at the books in your stupid cousin's bookcase? she said. Not a single decent novel, not one book of poetry, no plays, no biographies, no history, no philosophy. It's all jewellery catalogues and craft books. It's all how-to books. Nothing there to reflect the varieties of human experience. But Ariadne, I said, I know for a fact that he is an extraordinarily well-read person. The only experience he cares about is his own experience, she said. He wants everything to be his way, not your way, or anyone else's way, just his way. That's why your stupid cousin is stupid, she said. That's the way he thinks you keep a family together. You tyrannize them. He sees the family breaking apart and he thinks: I can keep it together if everyone just follows orders, my orders. And when you don't follow orders, he abandons you. That poor little cat of your mother's cost over one thousand dollars in the end. Did you know that? Did you know that your stupid cousin gets up early in the morning and eats bowl after bowl of Red River Cereal. I saw him do this, she said. I saw him sneaking into the kitchen and eating his guilty bowl of Red River Cereal. He's got all that money and he can't even shit! And you know why? He's stopped up inside. He's constipated by the life he's led. Your stupid cousin has got all those brains and all that creativity and it can't flow out. He can't let go of it. That's why he's stupid. Ariadne, I said, just because the guy likes Red River Cereal. That doesn't prove anything. I like Red River Cereal. I like what it does for me. It's real Canadian. I like it a lot. He could have done so much with his life, he could have gone into science and made discoveries, he could have gone into government and organized systems, he could have done something new for the country of Canada, he could have figured things out. He's one of the few people I've ever met with that kind of ability, he could have done almost anything with that brain of his. But it never occurred to him, at least not seriously, to do anything with that brain of his except to make money and hold onto it. And you know why? Because he hasn't got any heart. A brain without a heart is a useless thing. You can have the biggest brain in the world, but you're just a dickhead if you haven't got heart. It's heart that keeps a family together. A family without heart is despicable. He's got heart, I said, he dragged my mother out of the mire dozens of times, he took care of all kinds of things. Your mother, she said. When you first told me about your mother, I thought you were exaggerating. But you were not. She is indeed a special case among mothers. She is heartless. She is mean. She is a killer. Your family is a heartless family. That's why they're trying to break you, because you have heart. Just like your father. And he died of a heart attack for Christ's sake! Think about it. Your grandmother had heart too and they're *still* scared to death of her. She saw you and she knew that in such a family you would need help. That's why she left you that property. Your family couldn't stand that. Your stupid constipated cousin couldn't stand that. He was jealous of you, although he could never admit it, not even to himself. He couldn't stand it that you got that property and he can't stand it that you've gone ahead and had a career as an artist. But he doesn't give a good shit about my career, I said. He is jealous of your career, she replied. You went a different way, your *own* way, not his way, and that is unforgivable to him. Those fabulous girls of his went a different way too, their own way. And they will never be forgiven either. Everyone finally went their own way. Even the cat went its own way, she said. And yet he persists in trying to control everyone. That is what I call a stupid man. He's not stupid, I said, he's brilliant. You went your own way, she repeated. You are the artist, the outsider—the artist in the family is always the outsider. *You sleep with the big cats.* Your stupid cousin does not sleep with the big cats. He heard the big cats growl. But he refused the call. He was too busy building up his wall of money to keep the big cats out. He wouldn't listen. He stuffed his ears with money. And now he can't even listen to music. He's so clean, your stupid cousin, so fastidious, that pink scrubbed shiny skin of his, clean like a big chubby baby is clean, she said. All that light, all those glittering jewels, she said, all that brilliant light. There is too much light. And your mother is harbouring all the darkness. Your stupid cousin wants to capture and preserve the light with his jewels. He cherishes the light down there in the basement. At night he goes down to the sepulchre, and puts on his eyepiece to magnify the light. He holds the light in his hand. That's what all this business is about.

The darkness is somewhere far away in the psychiatric hospital. You are light and dark. That's what your stupid cousin hates about you. It negates him. Your darkness is not confined to the psychiatric hospital. It flows everywhere. You make your living from your darkness. That's what every artist does. And it frightens him and he runs down to the basement and stares at those glittering points of light. I saw the big cats today. I left the barbaric rodeo and went to see the big cats at the Wild Kingdom in the desert. Lions, tigers, panthers, cheetahs. That couple who run the Wild Kingdom get along fine with the big cats. They live with the big cats. When the big cats had cubs, that couple slept inside the compound for two months. They risked their lives so that the big cats would accept them, let them become part of the pride, part of the family. Any night the big cats might have torn them apart. But they won the trust of the big cats. They became one with the big cats. Those people at the Wild Kingdom live in harmony with the darkness. Those people have heart. Those people are heroes. Not like the mean little shits at the rodeo. They hate the animals at the rodeo. The way they bang those animals around—it's so cruel and horrible—every one of these animals needs major chiropractic work after those shows, you should see what they do to them, it's just terrible, and I'm sorry, as romantic as the rodeo might seem, it's just some cruel fucking way to wrestle the animal spirit and cripple it and throw it to the ground, that's all it's about. It is not heroic to mangle dumb animals. *There is no heroic journey in that. There is no trip to the heart of the labyrinth to confront the monster.* These are just poor animals in the rodeo. They treat them as if they were monsters, but they are just animals. They put them out there, they grab them by the neck, they throw them down, they jump on them, they cripple them. These rodeo guys, they're no fucking heroes, these mean little bastards with their little pointy prick cowboy boots. It's all in their heads. The labyrinth is in their heads. They are all like my ex-husband Dexter. He wore those pointy little prick cowboy boots. And he thought when he married me that he had a beast that he could throw to the ground, he thought that he could tie me up and cripple me, she said. He thought I was his property, his livestock. I hate that bastard, that cowboy bastard. I'll never forgive him, never. You don't tie up the big cats. You sleep with the big cats. Animals are very nice—all they care about is that you exhibit the right behaviour—wag your tail, you know. And he thought when he married me that he was throwing the beast to the ground. Well I showed him a thing or two, and that family of his. I showed them a whole thing or two—about how to handle the beast—there ain't no way to do it—*the beast is wild and free and she just walks out on the rodeo and she does not have any regrets and she does not belong to anybody!* You know my great-grandfather was a giant, probably six foot seven, he was a titan, and he had to marry a woman that was right off the Mongolian plains. She was the only woman who was wild enough for him—*so don't ever, ever try to tie me up*, that's all I have to say to you.

I'm not sure I follow you, Ariadne, I said.

Phone somebody up and get them to cut the lawn, she said. And don't you go into London Ontario and cut the lawn. You weren't thinking of going in there to cut the lawn were you? asked Ariadne. Oh heck no, I lied. Good, she said. You can't go there without me. You'll have an accident. When you're in London Ontario I'm the driver. I'm glad you didn't kill that cat. I'll call you tomorrow. Don't ever kill a cat. Ariadne closed off. I tried not to think about the cat. Instead I reached into the pocket of my greenjeans and extracted the letter from Robert Crow, the neighbour, the letter that had re-entered my house, and placed it on the kitchen table. I ironed it with the palm of my hand and continued to read: *I fully intend to complain to the city authorities if this problem with your mother's property continues. I would appreciate it if you would make arrangements immediately to have the property maintained. The neighbours and my wife and I have become very upset about this whole situation.* It seemed to me that Bob, introducing such emotional elements, might have properly initiated a new paragraph at this point, but instead he heedlessly plunged on. This delinquent paragraphing irritated me. I took the letter that had ruined my day into the bathroom, tore it into several pieces and threw it into the toilet. I watched words and paper drift on the water for a moment and become still. *Care. Someone. Pleasure. Property.* That fucking cat, I said to myself. My mother and that fucking cat. How could I decree the termination of an unsuspecting creature that had the bad luck of getting involved with my mother? That cat is in a cat hotel, said my brilliant cousin, running up a monstrous tab. He said: Put that cat to sleep and cut your losses. I said: I will not kill the cat. He said: I advise you to put the cat to sleep. I said: I will not kill the cat. He said: You are making a bad decision. I said: What is the cat's name? He said: I don't know. *At least that cat is still alive,* I reflected, staring into the toilet at the remains of the letter that had twice entered my home. At least that cat survived my mother and my brilliant cousin. That cat did better than my poor brother, not to mention my poor physician father, I reflected. My brilliant cousin wanted me to kill a cat, a cat that I had never seen, a poor stray that used to hang around my mother's house. It was not my cat, but I was supposed to kill it. It was not my property. It was not my mother's property. It was nobody's property. It was not property. It was a cat. It was an innocent stray that had the misfortune of coming under the influence of my mother. When my mother began her annual sojourn at the psychiatric hospital, one of her friends, one of her helpful chums, phoned the Humane Society and got that cat a suite in the Cat Hilton. That cat was at the Cat Hilton running up a monstrous tab. My mother was at Club Demento running up a monstrous tab. It probably looked good to that cat: free food, nice company, exercise equipment, lots of time to sleep. It didn't look like death row to that cat. Perhaps it looked good to my mother, too, for similar reasons. That cat thought he had it made, he didn't know that he was only a phone call away from a snuff job. As for my mother, I don't know what she thought. The truth is I did know. She thought, for some reason, that she had killed that cat. But she had not. I also know she thought that she killed my brother. And perhaps she did. And I know she thought that she killed my father. And perhaps she didn't. But she definitely did not kill that cat. In the end that cat cost one thousand dollars to bail out. In the end I lost track of my mother altogether. And so I saved the cat and lost my mother, I reflected as I stared into the toilet. In truth I don't care at all about that cat, I reflected. If that cat were squashed by some anonymous bus or garbage truck, it wouldn't bother me in the least. Thousands of people are mangled every day in torture chambers, thousands of people every day are butchered in wars, slaughtered in highway accidents, annihilated in natural disasters, exterminated by incurable viruses, blown away in their own suburban homes—I can hardly be expected to care deeply about some marginal pussycat. And yet I fought for that cat's life. That's how things always go with my mother, I reflected, as I stared at the bits and pieces of Bob Crow's letter lolling in the water of my toilet, you wind up fighting the wrong battles, on the wrong battlefields, over the wrong issues—you wind up fighting for the cat. The truth is my brilliant cousin had no interest in that cat either. He was just creating another diversion. That's how things go with my brilliant cousin. He diverts you and diverts you and eventually you lose your sense of direction and you lie down for a rest and suddenly you realize he is standing above you with his foot on your face. The truth is I am glad I saved that cat, the cat my mother thought she had killed. The truth is my brilliant cousin could have killed that cat himself. He didn't even have to consult me. He had power of attorney, too. But he didn't want to commit felicide. He wanted me to commit felicide. But I did not commit felicide. The truth is he wanted me to commit *suicide*. He did not really want me to commit suicide, he just wanted me to roll over and play dead. There were so many diversions during those three anguished weeks, I reflected, as I gazed into my toilet. After a day of lixiviating my house in London Ontario, the house left to me by my grandmother, the house in which my currently missing mother holds a life interest, after a day of digging through the papers, moving through the clouds of dust and dirt, scraping off the filth and shit, filling up garbage bags with the greeting cards, photographs and death certificates, Ariadne would drive me to my brilliant cousin's house in the distant suburbs. He would lean back in his La-Z-Boy and create diversions. *By the way*, he would begin, and lo and behold there would be a new diversion which would waste a morning or a day or more. Absent savings bonds, missing pension cheques, a certain piece of jewellery or furniture that had belonged to the family, a trip to the safety deposit boxes. *By the way*, he said, as he leaned back in his La-Z-Boy, you cannot just indiscriminately stuff everything in garbage bags—after we had finally, after many days, stuffed most of it in garbage bags. There is much valuable property there for the family archives. You are responsible for that. You have to rescue that property. Of course, I said, how could I be so thoughtless? The family archives! And so for the next several days we emptied the revolting contents of the garbage bags and sorted and collocated and classified it for the family archives. How do we figure out what to keep and what to throw out? asked Ariadne. I don't know, I said. If this rotting garbage is so precious, if it's such a treasure, asked Ariadne, why has everyone just let it sit here for the last fifty years? I don't know, I said. Finally, after several days, we had it all organized and categorized in what I considered archival fashion. Ariadne asked: Just exactly where are the family archives located? I don't know, I said. Just where are the family archives? I asked my brilliant cousin. He leaned back in his La-Z-Boy and began to speak about opals, about how certain pressures in the earth create glittering opals. Australia is a good place to find opals, he said. As he talked about opals I became fascinated. I forgot about the family archives. He took us down to his basement and showed us tray after tray of luminescent opals, green and blue and fiery red. He had a personal relationship with each stone, its origin, its formation, its value. What a brilliant guy he was. The truth is, I reflected before my toilet, my brilliant cousin didn't give a shit about the family archives. *By the way*, he would begin leaning back in his La-Z-Boy, and then a new diversion. *By the way.* Late each afternoon Ariadne and I would stop at the psychiatric hospital to see my mother and then we would find our way to the house of my brilliant cousin in the distant suburbs where he would lean back in his La-Z-Boy. He had invited us to stay at his house in the distant suburbs while we cleaned my property and made it saleable. He had insisted. What a generous guy, my brilliant cousin. The truth is, I reflected, that he invited us because he was lonely. The truth is that he is alone. No one is hanging around at the house of my brilliant cousin, not friends, not family, if the truth be known. Except his wife, a woman who keeps busy. The truth is that he needed someone who appreciated his brilliance. Someone like me. *The truth is that he needed me around, because he had a plan for my property in London Ontario, and I was part of his plan, but it was not the same plan that I had for my property in London Ontario. It was a similar plan, but it was not the same plan.* And so over those three wretched weeks Ariadne and I cleaned my house on the devious street known as Blackpool Drive to make it saleable and at night we slept in the distant suburbs. And we called in Don the real-estate guy. And we put the house on the market. And we kept on cleaning. That a house could contain that much crap was a constant source of amazement to me. The door of that house was a mouth that had devoured steadily for generations, but in the end, the house, my house, suffered a terrible case of indigestion and vomited its entire contents in three execrable weeks. And one day Don the real-estate guy showed up with an offer, a decent offer. Someone wanted to buy my property, the property left to me by my grandmother, the house legally occupied by my mother, who was then in the psychiatric hospital, and is now somewhere. My house was saleable. We went to the house of my brilliant cousin that night, and told him that there was a decent offer. I was exhausted, I was happy, I had navigated the twists and turns. I was at the end of the journey. I was at the heart of things. My brilliant cousin congratulated me. He leaned back in his La-Z-Boy and began to talk about diamonds, about how you cut diamonds, how you sort diamonds, how you sell them; he discoursed about diamonds for several hours, he took us down in the basement and he showed us his diamonds, hundreds of shimmering stones, I listened stunned at his continuing brilliance, exhausted by it, hypnotized. And then just as he finished his dissection of diamonds, just before bedtime, we went back upstairs and he got into his La-Z-Boy one last time. BY THE WAY, said my brilliant cousin, and then he paused and leaned forward in his La-Z-Boy. By the way, he said, we have to set up a little contract regarding the property. It's a minor detail. That's how it is when you deal with a guy like my brilliant cousin, I reflected, as I stared into my toilet one year later, you have to keep taking care of certain minor by-the-way kind of details. No big deal, said my brilliant cousin. When you sell the property you simply replace it with a guaranteed equivalent. It's a normal procedure, said my brilliant cousin. You have to guarantee your mother's living arrangements for the rest of her life, said my brilliant cousin. *That's what a life interest is all about.* No problem, I said, I am happy to do that, I said. And I was, I reflected, as I stared into my toilet. After all, my mother brought me into the world and I'm grateful for that. She brought me into the world and fattened me up and then tried to kill me. And, continued my brilliant cousin, you must put up security in order to back up the guarantee of your mother's living arrangements, specifically you have to put up your property in Vancouver, he continued. Your mother will, in essence, hold the mortgage on your property in Vancouver. That is the way I read Grandma's will, said my brilliant cousin, that's what a life interest means, it means that your mother gets either a comparable alternate abode or the guaranteed use of the proceeds of the sale of the house, he continued. So, said my brilliant cousin, I'm going to draw up a little contract and you will put up your property in Vancouver as security. That's the way it's done. You will make a contract with your mother. Ariadne must sign too of course. And if you fail to fulfil your commitment, your mother has the right as mortgager to seize your property in Vancouver. As he spoke, I found myself getting sleepy. I was ready for bed. I struggled to stay awake. I struggled to think. I knew something critical was underway, and yet all I really wanted to do was sleep. Let me get this straight, I mumbled to my brilliant cousin, if I sell my property in London in order to pay off my house in Vancouver and give my mother an income, and if I fail to fulfil the contract which you are going to draw up for me, I could end up losing our property in Vancouver. That's the bottom line, he said, that's the bottom line. Why didn't you mention this little detail before? I asked, yawning. My brilliant cousin chuckled. I was getting around to it, but I wanted to present it at the right time. I said: I don't want to do that. I don't want to put up my Vancouver property. *You have no choice*, he said. I have given my word, I said, that I will pay my mother a good income for the rest of her life, I will sign an agreement to do so, but I will not enter a contract with my mother that puts my property in Vancouver at risk. That's just stupid, I said. My mother is a dangerous woman. One does not enter into that kind of deal with a person like my mother. Do you think I'm crazy? I'm not doing that. *You must do it*, he said, it was the intention of your grandmother's will. I won't do it, I said. He chuckled again. Well, said my brilliant cousin, I know how you feel about your mother, and I agree that she is a difficult case, and frankly I wouldn't let her hold a mortgage on my property either, and luckily there is a viable alternative, a preferable alternative: you will place the money from the sale of the house in a trust fund for your mother. And everybody lives happily ever after. I won't do that either, I said. I plan to use that money to pay off my house in Vancouver. *You have no choice*, he said. But that is not the right dream, I said to my brilliant cousin. You know about my dream. My dream is that I sell my property in London, give some of the proceeds to my mother, pay off my house in Vancouver, and give her money every month with the money I saved on the mortgage. But, said my brilliant cousin, you don't understand what you're asking of me. I have power of attorney, he said, I am legally obligated to your mother. I am a trustee. *If you should misappropriate your mother's funds*, I, as power of attorney, would be legally obligated to replace them, said my brilliant cousin. I can hardly be expected, said my brilliant cousin, to put myself at that kind of risk, can I? Then why don't you withdraw from the power of attorney? I said to my brilliant cousin, and then you won't be at risk. I am not in a position to do that, said my brilliant cousin. This doesn't seem right to me, I said, it is my property, after all. Not exactly, said my brilliant cousin. In a sense it's really your mother's property. That is what a life interest means. If it's my mother's property, I asked, why is it in my name? Why did Grandma will it to me? My brilliant cousin turned to Ariadne, is he always this stubborn? he asked. Ariadne looked at him

impassively and did not reply. My brilliant cousin turned back
to me. Don't forget my power of attorney, he said, you can't make
a move without me. You either sign the contract that I will draw
up or you put the money in a trust. You are about to be fucked,
said my brilliant cousin, in the bum. He did not really say this,
and yet he did, but I was not ready to hear it anyway, not yet, I
reflected, as I stared into my Vancouver toilet one year later, I
was not yet prepared to lose my faith in my brilliant cousin, my
surrogate father, who taught me to sail as a kid, who took me on
camping trips and gave me tips on the stock market, who helped
my mother on a hundred occasions, and who once even lent me
a suit to wear at a funeral. So what's it gonna be, my brilliant
cousin said to me, the contract or the trust? I did not reply. I felt
confused, lost, sleepy, and sadly, somewhat titillated. I was, after
all, on the verge of being violated. There was a long silence out
there in the distant suburbs, which was finally broken by the wife
of my brilliant cousin. Why did you tell them so soon dear? she
said, as if we weren't there. Why didn't you wait until they had
finished cleaning the house? That was her only comment of the
evening. My brilliant cousin chuckled for a moment and said,
why don't we all go out and have Chinese food tomorrow night?
There was a silence. I looked at Ariadne. She looked back with
an eerie knowing smile. It was that smile that saved me. It was
a smile that said: You can find your way out of this if you want
to. It was a smile that startled me. I began to wake up. *I am not*

going to sell the house, I announced, surprising myself. Ariadne continued to smile. There was a silence. *You have no choice,* said my brilliant cousin. I am not going to sell the house, I repeated. You have no choice, he repeated, a bit nervously. It's my property, I said, and if I don't want to sell it, I won't sell it. But, said my brilliant cousin, that's not what Grandma's will intended, she intended that your mother have use of the house or its proceeds. I don't agree, I said, Grandma gave me that property because she wanted me to control it. And my poor brother. And he is not here. She gave it to us, not to mother and not to you. She knew we were the best ones to make decisions about that property, not my mother, and not you. And I have decided not to sell it, I said. My brother and I have decided not to sell, I said. It's mine. It's my property. It's been my property for many years. The way I understand it, if one owns property in this society, one generally has the right not to sell it. But you've put the house on the market, you have an offer, said my brilliant cousin. You and Ariadne have done all this work to make it saleable. *You have to sell,* he insisted. I won't sell, I said. I *choose* not to sell, I said. The game is over, I said. You will sell the house, he said. No I won't, I said. My brilliant cousin got up out of his La-Z-Boy. Like many artists, he said, you have a tendency to tilt at windmills. But let me assure you, there are no monsters in this household. We, my wife and I, are your friends, he said. We are trying to do what's best for you. And then my brilliant cousin went to bed. The next morning, Ariadne and I moved out of my brilliant cousin's house in the distant suburbs and went to see a lawyer. The lawyer explained what a power of attorney was and what a life interest was. My brilliant cousin had misled me, more or less, said the lawyer. And yet he had also told the truth, more or less, said the lawyer. He had interpreted the law in a rational way, but his interpretations were somewhat inventive, said the lawyer. The lawyer, who knew of my brilliant cousin, said that my brilliant cousin was a respected businessman in London Ontario, a little tight with his money, but honest and real smart, not a guy to tangle with. He was a bit nervous when he said this. I asked the lawyer if I could sell the house without the approval of my brilliant cousin. Yes and no, he said, you can sell it, but there could be legal complications. That is to say, I think you're pretty safe, on the other hand, there are dangers. I asked the lawyer to draw up an agreement between me and my mother in which I would agree to pay my mother a handsome income after the sale of the house and in turn she would agree to let me sell it without encumbrance. He drew it up and said: You know, of course, this agreement is worthless. I thanked the lawyer for clarifying the situation. As we were leaving he added, you know if the price is right, I might be interested in that property myself. What a sweet guy, I thought. I took my agreement to the psychiatric hospital and presented it to my mother who refused to sign for fear of offending my brilliant cousin. And who can blame her? After all my brilliant cousin had made her a lot of money. He had taken her meagre savings and invested them and worked a miracle. Here was a woman who had never done a day's work in her life and she had over a hundred thousand in the bank. I don't blame her at all. I mean the guy is brilliant. Better to offend the son, than risk offending someone like that. So much for my legal agreement with my mother. Some time later the lawyer sent me a bill for two hundred dollars. And who can blame him? The curious thing is that if my brilliant cousin had been straight with me from the beginning, I reflected, as I stared into my Vancouver toilet at the remains of the letter that had ruined my day, I would simply have accepted his counsel as I always had before, and signed his contract or set up the trust fund and then tried to find my way out of London Ontario. I have always had complete confidence in my brilliant cousin. But when I realized that he was not straight, when I realized that he had misled me, more or less, when I realized that by following his directions *I had gotten lost in London Ontario*, I knew that I had to go my own way. I knew instinctively that if I did not there would be still more surprises among the twists and turns and I would get so badly lost in London Ontario that I would never get out. The curious thing is *I don't give a shit about that property*. And neither does my brilliant cousin. What he really gives a shit about is manipulating the deal, calling the shots, controlling the sequence of events, taking charge of things. My brilliant cousin likes to push the buttons. When he controls the deal, he feels real, he feels that he is a god, the god of the deal. Sometimes he gets you to sign his deal willingly, sometimes he beguiles you, sometimes he bullies you, I reflected. And for my brilliant cousin, every human transaction finally boils down to the deal. And it's always the same deal—his deal. This is the essence of my brilliant cousin's life. These reflections put me in mind of a certain visiting professor from Boston, an admired and respected director who stayed with us for a time in Vancouver, who brought an endless succession of women to the house, usually his students, and fucked them. Ariadne and I could hear him through the walls groaning and grunting as he worked on his nightly fuck. No matter what woman he was fucking, rich or poor, dead or alive, it always sounded like precisely the same fuck. He fucked and fucked, but the cycle of his passion, or whatever it was, was always the same. And, I reflected, I was just another fuck for my brilliant cousin. And I resented it. Can you blame me? And so I did not sell the property. The deal was not consummated. And now the house just sits there the lawn just grows and my mother has disappeared and my brilliant cousin has gone on to new deals. And as I stood in my bathroom one year later looking into my toilet and thinking of my brilliant cousin, thinking about the lawn and my property and the CBC and the big cats, I was momentarily overcome with a desire to fly to London Ontario, take a cab over to the house of my brilliant cousin and hit him in the face with some common implement such as a baseball bat or a brick, and then afterwards take another cab over to my property and cut the lawn. I reached out and violently flushed the toilet. I watched the remains of Robert Crow's letter swirl through the waters and disappear. I immediately regretted my rash action, for I had not finished the letter and I was curious about its conclusion. But it was now irretrievable. However, one scrap had adhered to the moist declivity of the bowl. I leaned in and picked it up. *ur mother*, it read, *but not until*. I threw it back into the toilet where it floated alone on the rising water of the now replenishing bowl. The gentle motion of the water brought peace to my heart. And although I regretted its premature disappearance, the watery fate of Robert Crow's letter left me tranquil. For a moment, I wistfully recalled an incandescent morning long ago when my brilliant cousin took me sailing on the gilded waters of Georgian Bay. I recalled being happy. My brilliant cousin wasn't such a bad guy, I reflected, as the liquid found its proper level. The truth is, he's a good guy. In his own mind he was trying to do the right thing, I reflected. My brilliant cousin simply didn't trust me, I reflected. And who can blame him? The gerontological press constantly carries cautionary items about ungrateful sons and daughters who persuade Mom and Dad to sell the family property and then steal their money. They lie and mislead their parents, saying that they will care for them with the money. Then as soon as they've got their sticky little hands on the cash, they unload the unsuspecting old ones in some second-rate seniors' dorm where they rot and die with their hearts broken and their illusions shattered. It happens every day, according to the gerontological press. Perhaps, in his own mind, my brilliant cousin wanted to save my mother, currently missing, from such a fate. Perhaps that is how he rationalized it when he manipulated me and more or less misled me and in the end prevented me from setting her up in some nice apartment to live out her sunset years, as they call them in the gerontological press, a place where she could prepare for a dignified death, as they call it in the gerontological press. My brilliant cousin achieved the precise opposite of what he intended to achieve. And so did I. Both of us victims of Mom's First Law. He forced my hand and I played my pathetic ace: I chose not to sell. My brilliant cousin tried to persuade me that it was really *not* my property, but in the end it turned out that it really *was* my property. My brilliant cousin said that I had no choice, but in the end it turned out that I did have a choice. And I made my choice. And I did not sell. And I took the property off the market. And Ariadne and I finished the cleaning. And I went to the psychiatric hospital one last time, and I said goodbye to my mother. She did not say goodbye to me. Then Ariadne drove me through the distorted streets of London Ontario and took me beyond the city limits and kept on going straight down the 401 to the Toronto airport. It's over I thought as the 767 flew west towards the dark mountains. I have escaped, I thought. I am still alive, I thought. And, one year later, as I regarded the final fragment of paper suspended on the clear waters of my toilet, I reflected that Canada is a big country. There is room to escape in Canada. People are always escaping in Canada, I reflected. The whole country is filled with escape artists, I reflected. That is the history of Canada, I reflected. That is the thing I love about Canada. If I were living in a small country, say Iceland or Luxembourg or Austria, where there is no room to escape, I would have sucked back a cup of Drano years ago, I reflected as I gazed into the depths of my toilet. But with the help of Ariadne I made good my escape to the Vancouver hideout on the edge of the Pacific. It is over, I thought. But it was not over. It was not a clean escape. Some part of me was still gridlocked in London Ontario. And one day last fall when I was directing an opera, *The Man Who Mistook His Wife for a Hat*, which happened to be about mental illness, a special delivery packet rocketed through the mail slot. *My brilliant cousin had decided to sell my house!* He had engaged a real-estate agent who had shown the property, my property, to prospective property purchasers. Strangers were running around my house, the house legally occupied by my missing mother, the garbage-free house that I left behind in London Ontario. My brilliant cousin's packet included an offer from a prospective purchaser, who not only wanted the house, but also proposed that I throw in my poor destroyed baby grand.

My brilliant cousin strongly advised me to accept this offer; and true to form, my brilliant cousin had added a number of threats, which I can no longer remember, mainly about turning my mother over to the public trustee, and that kind of thing, if I did not accept this offer. I wonder how my brilliant cousin would like it if I entered the squiggly streets of London Ontario and put his house up for sale, I thought to myself, as I stared into the toilet, I wonder if he would be amused at having dirty buyers tracking their filth all over his property, I wonder if he would like to hear threats about what I might do to his mother, I reflected. I reached out and flushed the last remnant of Robert Crow's letter down the toilet, remembering the mixture of pleasure and fear I experienced in the fall when I similarly tore and then flushed the special-delivery packet from my brilliant cousin that contained that churlish offer for my property. No one is selling my property, I reflected. It is mine, I said to myself, mine, I repeated, as I stared into the unobstructed waters. Mine. I own a house that I do not want, I reflected, I have a lawn that I do not cut, I reflected, I have a mother that I cannot find, I reflected. Absurd, I reflected. I am an absurd person I reflected, an absurd person from an absurd family. The family itself is an absurd institution, I reflected. To be born into a family places one in an absurd situation. You are born helpless and the family feeds you and the family wipes your ass. Then just when you get used to this, and accept it as reality, the family tells you to feed yourself and wipe your own ass. And so you get used to this too, and then the family tells you to go to school where you encounter boredom brutality and lies served out by barely educated block-heads who have the audacity to call themselves teachers. Time passes and you realize that you are expected to undertake certain duties and responsibilities, which if undertaken will destroy your mind, your spirit and your very existence. You fight, you rebel, you flee, and perhaps you escape, at least you think you escape, but you do not escape. For one day the letter comes in through the mail slot and plops onto the floor reminding you that nothing has changed, that you are still absurd, that you were born absurd and that someday you will die absurd. You think someday that it will end, that you will grow up, and that you will be an adult, and that the family will treat you like an adult, but you never grow up, you are always a child, you have lived the life of a child, an absurd child, and someday you will die your death like a child. You were born in a hospital where they wiped your ass, and someday you will die in a hospital where they will once again wipe your ass, and in between those wipes of the ass you wiped your own ass but no one really gave you credit for it. You are still a dirty-ass little brat as far as your so-called loved ones are concerned. You want to do the right thing, but it is not the right thing, you cannot do the right thing by definition, you cannot wipe your ass, at least not properly, you are a failure at wiping your ass. You could show them Polaroids of your asshole,

perfectly wiped, and they would say: *Who did that for you?* And
if in spite of it all, you do something with your life, you find a way
to live, and survive and perhaps even to make a contribution of
some kind, they spit on you for your success, they find you
intolerable, even hateful, they would prefer it if you were dead,
they would prefer to murder you, or better, they would prefer you
to commit suicide, like my poor brother who one night, after a
mysterious incident with my mother, recognized the absurdity,
the permanent absurdity of his circumstances, and threw himself
under the wheels of a train. And the family liked it that way.
They were delighted. At the funeral they were positively jolly.
They went to a great deal of trouble over the seating arrangements, about who should sit directly in front of the coffin and
who should sit in the front row and the second row. They
actually took my mother by the arm and manhandled her into
what they considered the appropriate chair. One of my cousins
took my arm in a firm grip and tried to manhandle me into the
appropriate chair. Even in the face of death they do not give up
control. I shook off his arm and he grabbed me again. I quietly
informed him that I would break his arm if he touched me again.
He was somewhat stunned by this and ran off to tell the others
of my boorish behaviour at my brother's funeral. He shoves me
around like a museum exhibit and gets offended when I resist.
And I would have broken his arm. I am capable of doing that
kind of thing, both temperamentally and physically. I have not

neglected my body. I am the only person in my deformed and disease-ridden family who has even noticed that he has a body. This is another reason they would like to see me dead. As a group they are an unusually ugly family. This is not a genetic characteristic, they have made themselves that way by chronically abusing and ignoring their bodies throughout their entire lives. This was never clearer to me than at the funeral of my poor brother. I looked at them and realized that they were all fat, some were obscenely fat, so fat that they could barely waddle out to their cars after the service, they were so fat as a group that their bodies threatened to burst out of their clothes spill over the folding chairs and spread great globules of puddled fat over the entire funeral home. I looked at this group that had come to my brother's funeral and could barely make out the outline of humanity in their distended forms, I looked at these jolly bulging funeral-goers and I almost vomited on the spot. I covered my mouth and struggled to control my vomiting reflex. They regard my slim athletic body with fear and contempt. They often speak to me about it. You are slim, they say, you are so slim, how do you do it, they ask, their voices filled with loathing. It's unhealthy they say. You'll hurt yourself with all that exercise. I am a traitor for being slim, for acknowledging that I have a body, for learning to move my arms and legs. When I was a young man and something of an athlete, a runner actually, they never came to see me in a single event. Of course nowadays they will not read my writing either. Perhaps it's just as well. And when my work is broadcast or performed they find that they are too busy to tune in or attend. Although, naturally, if I get a bad review, they are only too happy to tell me that they agree with it. I haven't had time to see your play, they say, but I think what the reviewer said sounds right. My brother, a promising young filmmaker, killed himself in the midst of this family and they gathered at his funeral to celebrate. And now each time one of them dies, I also celebrate, I buy a cigar and a bottle of champagne. And on the day my brilliant cousin dies, I will throw a party. But I will not go to his funeral. And I do not want him to come to mine. Or any of the other fatties that comprise my failed family. What a heinous enterprise a family is, I reflected. Not all families, of course, some rare families are delightful. Ariadne's family is delightful. But most are heinous. And this heinous enterprise, the family, is a fundamental unit of our society, I reflected. And property too is a heinous thing, I reflected, and property too is fundamental to our society, I reflected, as I stared into my toilet bowl. Family and property. And I turned away from my toilet bowl and walked back to the kitchen where I encountered, on the table, the forgotten envelope bearing the stamp of the Queen who resembles my mother, the envelope that had once contained Robert Crow's letter, the letter that had entered my house and ruined my day, the letter that I had not finished, the letter that I would never finish, the letter about my property in

London Ontario, the property legally occupied by my missing
mother. This is what it has all finally come to, I reflected bitterly,
a letter complaining about the deterioration of Grandma's
property, now mine, the property she left to me and my poor dead
brother, the property that I do not want but will not sell.
Perhaps, I reflected, if I could sell the deteriorating house, get rid
of it, perhaps then I could get rid of my deteriorating family. And
yet I do not really believe it. There are no simple solutions, I
reflected. Except death. The only thing that will really do the job
is death. The collective death of my family would do the job. As
would mine. And neither party is in a hurry to do the other a
favour on this score. And who can blame us? And so I will not
sell. I suspect now that my brilliant cousin would simply turn
away in disgust if I did, in fact, sell. The truth is that I could
probably now sell my property in London Ontario and pay off my
house in Vancouver and set up a nice income for my mother
wherever she is. But I will not sell. The truth is I could find my
mother if I made a few phone calls. I would simply have to phone
all the psychiatric hospitals in London Ontario and eventually
I would hit upon her current domicile. But I will not do that
either. What would I say to her? Hi Mom, it's me, how are you
feeling? As legal tenant of my property, you should have cut the
lawn this year, as specified in the Real-Estate Act of Ontario
(Real Property Law, 1983, pp. 8-9). Or would you rather give me
legal permission to sell the place so that you can have a nice

income for the rest of your life? No, I will not say these things. And I will not go to London Ontario and its squirming avenues and sell the house. I will not go there to cut the lawn. I am afraid to go to London Ontario. I am afraid to die. Instead I will let the house sit there on Blackpool Drive, a monument with its memorial lawn, a crumbling weed-strewn memento for my brilliant cousin, for my mad mother, for my tumid family and for all those who have lost their way in London Ontario. I will continue of course to pay the taxes so that I maintain control of my property and it will sit there like an oozing boil on Blackpool Drive envenoming the whole neighbourhood with its noxious toxin. Property values will decline. The nightmares of Bob Crow will become reality, he will sell his own property in despair, taking a major loss. Undesirable elements will buy in. A plague will spread, savaging the properties on the worm-like curves of Blackpool Drive. The captivating yards will turn dangerous as violence, crime and depravity ravage the bushes and flower beds. And all because it's my property and I do what I want with my property and what I want to do is *kill my property*. I want to kill my property, I repeated. I am no better than my mother, I reflected. My mother was a killer. I am a killer, I reflected. This is the time of killers, I reflected. This is the century of killers. Our heroes are killers. Our politicians are killers. Our young people are killers. Our business people are killers. Our scientists are killers, our physicians are killers, our religious leaders are killers.

We are all killers. We kill in countless ways. We kill the plants, we kill the animals, we kill the earth we kill the air and kill the water and we kill each other and we kill ourselves and we kill God. We watch killing on the TV, and in the movies, and we read about it in our newspapers and periodicals. Killing is the major study of our time, the major occupation, the major obsession, the major hobby, the major amusement, the major everything. That is where we have put our energy. That is where we have put our money. We have done more killing in this century than in the rest of recorded history. My mother just wanted to get in on the action. And so do I. And who can blame us? Everybody's doing it. And most of the time they get away with it, I reflected. Take the instance of a man in Washington named Robert Martens who killed over one million people in Indonesia in 1965. He did this without leaving his office. He got away with it. He was promoted. His story is not unusual. And almost no one knows it, certainly not the vague Robert Crow who is worried about the lawn. Robert Martens compiled a list the size of a phone book, a list of American enemies, and he gave this list to an Indonesian named Achmed Sukarno, another killer, who systematically killed every man woman and child on the list and many many more. Achmed got away with it, too. When I consider such master killers as these, I am amazed that we even bother to jail those comparatively innocent serial killers who stalk our cities, modest inefficient murderers who take out their victims one at a time. My mother apparently sentenced herself to life in the psychiatric hospital, with occasional paroles, for what seem, in the larger context of the era, to be almost trivial infractions: a couple of alleged killings and an alleged attempted killing. But the truth is my mother's incarceration sprang from a far more majestic origin: *my mother caused World War II.* She came to this realization in the mid-forties. She announced that she had caused the war. No one believed her. And I don't blame them. After all, she was in London Ontario, a difficult place for a housewife with two small kids to begin a major European conflict. But she continued to proclaim her guilt to all who would listen. She had found a way into the action and she knew that she had to be punished for it. Finally, she turned herself in and received a session of corporal punishment in the form of electro-shock therapy, the first of many such punishments. I was not told of my mother's war crime until the time of my brother's death. My kind and brilliant cousin found it appropriate to regale me with this tale a few days after the funeral. No account of my mother's diverse psychiatric history ever affected me so deeply. For I realized with finality that my mother was indeed mad, or at least had been mad, and that she had likely been mad through most of my childhood, those years when she was supposedly bringing me up. And so after perpetrating her global crime, the petty peccadilloes that followed were indeed trivial and irrelevant. This well-educated and intelligent woman looked at the world and went mad. And, I reflected, *perhaps this is the correct response*. Perhaps it is madder to live out our primly-hedged daydreams and stare at the lawn while the world turns to shit around us, I reflected. Like many women, I reflected, my mother was shut out of the action, and she wanted in. She wanted to participate, so she started the war. She made herself part of the larger madness. She made herself part of the world. And she found her place in that world, she found the psychiatric hospital. She recognized that the psychiatric hospital was the proper sphere for worldly action, that it was precisely equivalent to those other institutions that make the world what it is. Perhaps in a different family, she would have been an artist, or a healer, or a teacher, but no one recognized that she had ability, or imagination, and so they married her off to raise the kids and rot, and she refused this domestic destiny and entered the great world through the back door of the psychiatric hospital, I reflected, holding the envelope that had once contained a complaint about my lawn. My mother is mad, I reflected, and she went mad after I was born, I reflected. The legal tenant of my property is mad, I reflected. The property itself is mad, I reflected. I am mad, I reflected. I am going mad, I reflected. I am in Vancouver, with its dark mountains, and I am mad, I reflected, staring at my envelope. And only death will cure my madness, and my mother's madness, and the madness of the world. And the three of us are well on our way, I reflected. What a bitter passage, I said to myself, what a bitter passage. And then I laughed out loud. For the truth was that in spite of the family, and my brilliant cousin, and the CBC, and the deviant streets of London Ontario, in spite of the betrayals and lies and killings, in spite of my property and the world and my crazy mother, in spite of Robert Crow and his letter-writing activities, in spite of the demons of guilt and regret, in spite of all, I believed it was still possible to have a good life. I am indeed mad, I reflected, holding up the envelope, in spite of all, I go on. I have Ariadne, and my work, and my students, I reflected, and I go on. And it can only end in nothing, and I go on. I have the theatre, I reflected, an institution not unlike the psychiatric hospital. And I go on. I have a home, still owned mainly by the bank. And I go on. I have the dark mountains, I said to myself, the dark mountains. And I go on. I have dreams. Some, like the hopeful dream of last summer, turn to shit, but others come true. And I go on. In the theatre, one can see dreams come true. That is why I am in the theatre. And I go on. And perhaps someday, I will go back to London Ontario and try again. I will go back to my property and cut the lawn and make it saleable, I will provide a decent income for my mother, and I will bail her out of the crazy house, and set her up in a nice apartment. And yes I know it won't work out, and something will go wrong, because something always goes wrong, every time, but my dream will be strong by that time, it will be irresistible, and I will go on, and perhaps I will get permanently lost in the twisting ever-twisting streets of London Ontario. And still I will go on. But perhaps, perhaps, I reflected, holding the envelope, just once I will make my dream come true.

The Author

Property is Marc Diamond's second novel. The first, *Momentum*, was published in 1985 by Arsenal Pulp Press in Canada and Penguin Books in the United States. He has also written a number of plays, with works performed in Canada, the United States, and England. He is active as a theatre director and has directed numerous contemporary plays and operas. He teaches at Simon Fraser University School for the Contemporary Arts in Vancouver.

Guest Editor: D.D. Kugler
Editor for the Press: Jason Sherman
Design: Shari Spier / Reactor
Cover Illustration: Henrik Drescher
Author Photo: Daniel Collins
Printed in Canada

Coach House Press
401 (rear) Huron Street
Toronto, Canada
M5S 2G5

Printed on paper
containing over 50%
recycled paper including
10% post-consumer fibre.

Printed in Canada